## Marie-Helene Bertino
## EXIT ZERO

Marie-Helene Bertino is the author of *Beautyland, Parakeet, 2 A.M. at The Cat's Pajamas*, and the story collection *Safe as Houses*. She was the 2017 Frank O'Connor International Short Story Fellow in Cork, Ireland. She has received the O. Henry Prize, the Pushcart Prize, the Iowa Short Fiction Award, the Mississippi Review Prize, and fellowships from Macdowell, Ragdale, Sewanee, and New York City's Center for Fiction, and her work has been included in *The Best American Short Stories 2024*. She is the Ritvo-Slifka Writer-in-Residence at Yale University and lives in Brooklyn with her partner, the poet Ted Dodson.

# EXIT ZERO

# EXIT ZERO

STORIES

## Marie-Helene Bertino

FSG ORIGINALS

FARRAR, STRAUS AND GIROUX  NEW YORK

FSG Originals
Farrar, Straus and Giroux
120 Broadway, New York 10271

Title-page art by Canicula / Shutterstock.com.

Library of Congress Cataloging-in-Publication Data
Names: Bertino, Marie-Helene, author.
Title: Exit zero : stories / Marie-Helene Bertino.
Other titles: Exit zero (Compilation) | Exit 0
Description: First edition. | New York : FSG Originals / Farrar, Straus and
    Giroux, 2025.
Identifiers: LCCN 2024039947 | ISBN 9780374616472 (paperback)
Subjects: LCGFT: Short stories.
Classification: LCC PS3602.E7683 E95 2025 | DDC 813/.6—dc23/
    eng/20240906
LC record available at https://lccn.loc.gov/2024039947

Designed by Abby Kagan

Our books may be purchased in bulk for promotional, educational, or business
use. Please contact your local bookseller or the Macmillan Corporate and
Premium Sales Department at 1-800-221-7945, extension 5442, or by email at
MacmillanSpecialMarkets@macmillan.com.

www.fsgoriginals.com • www.fsgbooks.com
Follow us on social media at @fsgoriginals and @fsgbooks

1  3  5  7  9  10  8  6  4  2

*For Claudia Ballard's lucky right ankle*

# Contents

# EXIT ZERO

# Marry the Sea

◯

This never happened.

A cargo ship unloading in New York Harbor drops a crate that cracks in two and explodes into thousands of pink and yellow parakeets. Some of them nest in Green-Wood Cemetery, in mausoleums with views of the Statue of Liberty. Some fly along the F to Coney Island, others follow the A to the Cloisters, still others the 7 to Woodside—where they settle in the trees of my mother's Queens neighborhood. They eschew other birds, preferring to circle around one another in flight like bright tornadoes. They are snooty and condescending. They side-eye me when I visit. Preen their feathers and judge.

Someone says, let's have a beach day. Let's bring blankets and cold salads and swim. Let's comment on how the boats look in the distance and ask one another for advice. I'll bring what I'm good at, you bring what you're good at. Get that girl who's good at everything to come. Will you come? You don't see why not. I'll drive unless you want to. I wish we were already there. Let's never die. Let's never not have fun again.

———

A woman lives on a ship docked in the Brooklyn Navy Yard. On the ship she has painted the words I AM DYING. On the other side: AND YOU ARE TOO. She doesn't leave the ship and she loathes visitors. If someone wants to visit, she yells, "Put it in writing!" Letters can be placed into a bucket that hangs from the bowsprit. I am going there tonight with a handwritten letter and a heart that churns as wildly as the blood-black sea.

I read somewhere that a hummingbird's heart beats 1,400 times a minute but there's no way that's true.

After surgery restores his vision, six-year-old James will wear a blindfold for weeks. His neurons must rewire and make new connections. His eyes will not have the graphs and borders that order light and color like lines in a coloring book. Encountering a tree for the first time post-surgery, James will see only what's reflecting off the leaves and trunk. Frightening, unorganized light.

The printer is broken. Girl meets boy when they are sent by their respective departments to look into it. They introduce themselves then turn to the task at hand. They begin to speak in the voice of the printer. "I am the world's most persnickety printer," girl says. "I have operatic-level needs." "Go 'head, fix me," boy says. "I'll wait until the most important meeting of your life to crap out again." In their representations, girl and boy agree the printer is a grumpy sort, with the hint of a Bronx accent. On their last go-around, the girl pantomimes a cigar. She's uncertain why she and the boy are acting this way, or at what point they should stop. Who are we, she thinks. What the fuck is going on?

I rescue a dragonfly from a spider's web using my car key. It is out of the fire, as it were, but the web has shrink-wrapped its left wing. It bats itself against the concrete, spiraling pointlessly. I bear witness. Is life very fragile or very resilient? This dragonfly's struggle scores one for both.

I visit the woman who lives on the ship that reads I AM DYING. Her skin and hair are grayed by the salt air's assault, as if she is becoming one of the canal boulders restraining the land so the ferries and ships can sing by. "Come down," I yell, hair whipping in my face. "Come up," she says. "There's no ladder," I say. She says, "Maybe not one you can see."

A photographer saunters over to where I am drying a mug and says, "How's the waitressing business?" "Fine," I say, "if it's okay with you to get things like this for a tip." I hold out a napkin where some meringue has written:

A HUMMINGBIRD'S HEART BEATS 1,400 TIMES A MINUTE.

"How is that even possible?" I say. "I think it's bullshit." The photographer says, "Someday, when you feel as pretty as you are, I'm going to take your picture." A camera dangles around his neck and he walks with a cane. His name is F. D. Reese Jr. I make him write it down.

My brother teaches me to make a fist. The first lesson is: Thumb goes outside not inside the hand. "That's a good way to break your thumb," he says.

Because I'm small, I'm a half-an-out girl. When I come to the plate, the pitcher yells *half an out!* to the shortstop, who repeats it to the outfield. So when I inevitably strike three, it won't cost anyone anything much. Except me, who has had to hear the idea of diminutiveness chorused out over the field as I swing. Smallness baffles the big; how it holds the same, often more, power.

"Hit me as hard as you can," my brother says. After preparing my fist, I do. My punch goes wobbly against his biceps. "Harder," he says. I make another fist, a better one, I hope. I want to cause him pain so he thinks I'm strong. "Harder!" A parakeet that had been watching surprises into the air. We cross the yard, pushed forward with every attack and reset. How violent. How full of love.

I return to the woman in the ship that reads AND YOU ARE TOO. I knock on the smooth, wide hull. I peer into a porthole. I ask the seagulls. I ask the angled, solemn moon. There is no answer. She is sleeping. On the concrete dock, I sleep too.

On three, girl and boy reveal their biggest on-the-job mistakes then make fun of each other's ruthlessly. His: miscopying a report so the finished product was comprised solely of page 90s.

Hers: serving spoiled cream to executives. They reveal scars on their bellies and legs. He says, "I can control dogs with my mind." She says, "I'm double-jointed like everywhere." She bends her thumb back to touch her arm and he focuses on a Pomeranian in a nearby booth. She says she was born being able to do this and he says, "Me too with the dog thing." Instead of a tip, they write the waitress a note on a napkin. It says: A HUMMINGBIRD'S HEART BEATS 1,400 TIMES A MINUTE.

Six-year-old James gives me directions to Saturn: make a left at Brooklyn, 95 south, fly over this cloud then that cloud, out through the atmosphere, quick left, you're there. "I'll go while you're in surgery," I say. "And tell you how it is." "Just be safe," he says. "There's a lot of there out there."

It's noon at the coffee shop. We're almost out of turkey. A writer is drunk at a table. She is telling people who aren't listening what she thinks about this writing stuff. Writers today should study architecture! Nabokov built houses for his readers! Each chapter a room. She says the problem with most novels is that too much happens. A novel should be as eventful as an instruction manual on how to read an instruction manual. Once upon a time is a dumb way to start a story. It's obvious and redundant and a lie.

A small bird lands on a tree outside the window by the writer's head. "Look," I say. "A parakeet."

"A parakeet?" she says. "A fucking parakeet?"

———

Some scientists believe if you place a virus into a petri dish of water then remove it, the water retains memory of the virus. This would mean that molecules can communicate with each other without being in physical contact. Other scientists contest this, consider the water memory scientists to be naive dreamers. Last night, I sat under the stars holding your ratty sweater against my cheek.

Sara Rice has cerebral palsy. I assumed because she had a disease she was a kind person, in the way we are all, when confronted by the headlights of death, prioritized. I introduced her to my friends, cooked her a meal from a centuries-old recipe. Sara Rice belittled my interests, hit on my boyfriend, ripped off my front bumper with her bare hands. I asked why she did it. She said she wanted to see if she could. Sara, I don't know where you are these days. I'm sorry I failed to imagine you.

The boy's penis had been injured in war and replaced with two orchids that needed different kinds of sunlight. The girl doesn't want a sexual relationship. She wants him to return home from running, mealy, happy, and raw, and accept a forkful of sausage she holds out without looking. How can she tell him *I want you to chew over my shoulder and ask what I'm reading*? No one believes you when you're honest. So she says, "I don't want a sexual relationship," and leaves the rest unsaid and he senses a withholding and assumes she's lying and she feels misunderstood and eventually they get into separate cars and part.

———

At a stoplight on a country road, the boy is observed by a deer in the tree line. After the boy passes, the deer plunges into the forest and gallops through the underbrush. It reaches a highway and leaps into the path of the girl's car. She swerves to avoid collision and ditches onto the muddy shoulder, heart beating ___ times a minute. The deer runs until it reaches a fern-soft glade. Where we see a bed of vegetation the deer sees deep cover. This is its home. It knows exactly where it is. The deer tucks its nose beneath its hind legs and dozes off against its sleeping mother.

"I got you a present," says the woman who lives in the ship. She tosses a ladder over the main deck. "So I climb this up to where you are." I am in disbelief. It seems too simple after so much distance. She nods. We each know what could be about to happen. I hold the first rung in my hands. It is ornery and strong, the way I'd guess a ladder leading up to her would be. I want to live in a ship and marry the sea. I climb the first rung, then the second. I climb all night.

"How was Saturn?" James says. "Great," I say. "It was?" He sounds suspicious. "So great." "You're lying," he says, trembling. "You didn't go." "I did," I insist. "I know you didn't," he says. "I gave you the wrong directions."

The owner of this coffee shop informs me he does not pay me to shoot the shit with friends or little boys or random photographers or other waitresses. It is hot. We are out of turkey, a fact I was conveying to the other waitress when he rapped me on the shoulder to remind me what he doesn't pay me for. The lunch rush hits. Hungry people shuffle in. I tell him I have to feed my meter. He glares, but nods. I doff my apron and walk outside. I get in my car. I drive to my mother's house. Hundreds of parakeets sitting on the electric wires roll their eyes as I walk by. "Just in time," my mother says, pulling a box of cookies from the cupboard. She holds a gingersnap over one eye. "They're making them much smaller than when I was a girl." "I left my job," I say. "I got in my car and drove away." "Well," she says. "We knew you weren't a waitress." We are silent. Outside, the parakeets are shushed in listening. Mother, why is it impossible to hold the feeling of happiness inside me? Through her gingersnap monocle, my mother regards me. "Sweetheart," she says. "The whole world's gone wrong."

# Edna in Rain

I was walking to Higher Grounds when the first one fell from the sky. A whirring sound preceded him so I was able to sidestep to avoid a direct blow. He hit the ground at a distressing angle.

"Kevin Groutmeyer," I said. "Are you okay?"

He was more than okay, living with his partner and their twin boys in Harrisburg, and I said: "Amazing! Harrisburg!"

Kevin Groutmeyer was the one who could do the thing where you flip the girl from the top to the bottom without letting go. This necessitates the upper body strength of a wrestler and the focus of a physicist. I demonstrated it to several girlfriends, using a salt shaker for the girl and a pepper shaker for the boy.

Kevin had what you would call liquid brown eyes and shoulders as wide as a meadow. For once, I thought, the right person turned out handsome.

We beamed and held hands as if we were about to gallop through a line of dancers.

"Look at you," I said.

He said, "Look at you!"

My town's chief bragging point is: *A short drive to everything!* But me, I like to walk. Arms akimbo. Toes out. Let the whole world come, as far as I'm concerned. I continued my walk to town, akimbo. No sooner had I turned onto Orange Street than BLAM. Marisa O'Donnell landed in a bush!

She and her wife live in Pittsburgh. No kids but not from lack of trying. "You know how things can be."

"I really do," I said.

"Show me anyone who ended up where they thought." She smiled in a wooden way, as if her manager was watching. Help me, her eyes seemed to say.

I remembered that when she was close to climax she'd yell, *Hoo boy, isn't that something?* How do you answer that? I kept my voice bright. "Sing it," I said.

I told her I was happy for her then said goodbye. It shook me seeing her, to tell you the truth. I quickened my pace. A whirring sound, and Brent Winegarten hit the lamppost and performed a controlled roll. Rico Denera butt-slid into the mailbox. He was the one who begged me to help him not hit me. I kept my face pleasant but I didn't stop.

No ignoring Bernie Greene! He ricocheted against a few trees and the side of Higher Grounds before landing in a heap near the door.

"Quite an entrance," I said.

He expressed no happiness to see me: This is the prerogative of ex-husbands. An English professor, he spent much of our short marriage correcting my grammar.

He and his wife live in Philadelphia with their two . . . yawns.

"You've done great," I said.

"Well . . ." he said.

"Well what?"

He said, "I've done well."

"Bernie," I said, "I'm just trying to get some fucking coffee."

My best friend Yuna owns Higher Grounds. "It's raining my ex-boyfriends," I told her.

"I noticed," she said, handing me a Mud Latte.

I told her about my morning and she told me her carrot plants were finally responding to fertilizer.

"Kevin Groutmeyer?" She leaned in. "Isn't he the one who can do that thing?"

"In the flesh," I said. The Mud Latte was lightening up my mood.

Her eyes grew wide. "You don't think you'll see Mike?"

"Mike?" I said. "No. Mike? No."

I breathed in and out. A woman at the condiment table shook sugar into her espresso. A hard knot formed in my gut.

When I was leaving Yuna called out, "If you see Nick Fredericks, tell him I said go scratch." She gave me a be-strong fist-cheer that I answered with a here-goes-nothing grimace. I pushed through the door to the outside.

What had been a drizzle had become a steady rain. One-night stands were falling now, along with boys I'd stared at in school who'd preferred girls the heft of paper clips. Whirs and grunts as so many freckled shinbones I had forgotten met with ground.

Sometimes I feel like God's favorite sitcom. I shouldered through this intimate precipitation, clutching my latte. A few collected on a bench near the library. I recognized that guy (Marcus? Mario?) who didn't believe in driver's licenses, and Gregory, who broke up with me because he was "tired." There, rubbing a welt on his ankle, was Nick Fredericks, who dumped Yuna before asking me to the prom. He was her only boyfriend before she got married. Her exes wouldn't make a decent sun-shower.

I envied her as I saluted them from across the street, but at me they glowered. A cold front. I remembered their phone messages, the flecks of hope in their voices.

I was the opposite of akimbo. I no longer wanted the world to come to me.

Let that be all, I hoped, reaching the woods near my house. I stepped into a clearing I didn't recognize. A large stone jutted out from the grass. A grave site. I turned and walked in the other direction. After a few minutes I stumbled into the same grave site. I ran. The grave again. The grave. I couldn't avoid it.

I knew he was buried in his family's plot several states away but believe me when I say this grave too was real. I placed my palms against the cold granite—into it chiseled the name MIKE RADISH, my second-grade boyfriend.

His parents divorced that year then conducted a mean-spirited custody battle over his sister and him. Yet Mike had remained unaffected by the fighting. Every Sunday he sang in church, his gaze fixed somewhere over the heads of our unworthy congregation. His mouth, arranged in a careful O, made every *Ave* perfect, as if lowering each one down on a delicate thread.

One afternoon in the rain, our soggy lunches bunched in our fists, we achieved a quick, harrowing kiss.

During the first few weeks of chemotherapy he still looked like Mike but gradually he began to swell. His blunt nose and heavily fringed eyes held their shapes but the terrain of his skin expanded as the chemicals pulled him taut. Then he stopped coming to school.

Before Mike, I didn't know kids could die. There was really no getting to me after that.

I left the only thing I had, my coffee cup, on his grave, and found the path. Finished, I thought with relief. I knew how a balloon must feel, fretless and buoyed from within. I wanted to get to my house, where the woods relent and there is nothing but sky. Maybe the sky would be a certain shade of green or contain a cloud formation that might set me on a line of thinking that could turn out to be important. The idea placed a crackle of energy into my elbows and knees. I removed outer layers: my parka, my hat, my cardigan.

That's when I saw the man sitting on my front step.

I live on a long road with just my house at the end so I was able to consider him for a long time as I walked. Slim hands. Delicate knees in pressed gray pants. Had I forgotten someone? He gave me an isn't-it-so-like-you-to-be-late look but I knew I had never met this man before this day. He was relentlessly smiling if there is such a thing. Like those days when you can't get away from the sun, even when you are inside negotiating a dry-cleaning bill, it shines and shines.

# Exit Zero

Before the ringing phone startles Jo into upsetting a stack of crackers she'd been matching to cheese, before the man asks for Josephine and she says, "No one calls me that," before he identifies himself as the executor of her father's will and inhales sharply as if bracing for collision, Jo sits at her kitchen table, listening to her landlord's children pretend to be astronauts. Two floors down in the courtyard, they've improvised robes for space suits. Her ritual is to eavesdrop for indications that the bigger two are excluding the little one. She likes to imagine herself interceding, hipping the bullied child while delivering admonishments to the bigger two. Today the children are getting along, so Jo enjoys an off-duty feeling. It is Sunday. She assumes her father is still alive in that she is not thinking of her father at all. After the phone rings and the crackers vault, the children yell, "Blast off!" and the executor, braced, delivers the news that her father is dead and had lived in New Jersey, in a house that is now hers.

The will is practical, matter-of-fact. The house is to be sold; her father cremated. Whatever money is left after funeral costs and whatever is left of him—cremains, the executor calls them— are hers. Cremains. New experience brings new vocabulary. An unseen force yanks Jo's shoulder blades, as if someone has smoothed her the way you would a bedsheet.

The worst of the news conveyed, the man relaxes into chat. "Rio Grande," he says, "is a one-strip-mall town. The Econo

Lodge is the only motel. The other side of the peninsula is Cape May where the beach is beautiful, even now, in midwinter. Exit Zero on the Parkway." He promises to leave the key in a lockbox hanging on the front door if she will go soon, like tomorrow. "It will be up to you to clear the contents of the house before it sells, and your father has a few..." She hears the nervous click of a pen. "... sensitive items. Will you have help? Siblings or..."

"Only child." Jo stares at the address on the pad of paper. She is an event planner for a national organization of doctors. Right now, one hundred cardiologists are beginning their initial descent into Miami for a drug conference. She has coordinated accommodations and activities for their free time: massages, art deco tours, twilight snorkeling. "I'll have to take a leave of absence at my job." She expects the executor to sympathize. She thinks she knows his character because he is the purveyor of news that produces immediate intimacy. He remains silent. "Sensitive items?"

"It's on a cul-de-sac," he says. "Please go soon, like tomorrow."

"They have famous fish tacos, don't they?" she says, meaning the town.

He says, "They have what?"


Jo follows the executor's directions four hours south to a marshland town overrun by cattails and spartina. She parks in front of her father's prim ranch-style house. Bright windows. Exhaust stews around the idling station wagon.

———

The workout resistance bands arranged next to his bed are a surprise, as are the razors in the medicine cabinet. A few of his hairs remain in the hollow of a blade. Coarse and black like hers. Jo closes the mirrored door. His bedspread, a halfhearted floral, is perforated by an array of precise divots, as if it has recently been the resting place for a constellation of stars. Later, Jo will pinpoint this moment as when she should have suspected. Instead, she ticks through a plan: She will empty one room each day. She will not take one thing—not one thing—home. She will not use her father's possessions to puzzle out an image of what his life looked like before he succumbed to the disease she hadn't known was hollowing out his kidneys. Professional cleaners will arrive in a week, the house will be put on the market, and Jo will rejoin her life in New York. Already her phone vibrates with messages from work.

The refrigerator contains several jars of apricot juice. Lined, labels out. Jo transfers them to the counter. No milk or crusted ends of butter. Only these jars.

The drawers are stuffed with brochures for zoos all over the world. A zookeeper's card is fastened to the fridge with a magnet for the Cape May Wildlife Association.

Jo jerks the chain for the pantry light and finds hundreds of boxes of matzo stacked in uniform rows. Apricot juice, zoo brochures, and matzo. Were these the sensitive items?

By the end of the day, the contents of her father's kitchen have been transferred into trash bags she bought at a Shop & Save. One week before, Jo did not know where her father lived. Now she is dragging the most delicate part of what kept him alive to the curb. The sun has retreated behind the water tower that reads: RIO GRANDE: A GREAT PLACE TO GET FROM HERE TO THERE! The false daylight of Atlantic City hovers behind it. Insert easy Jersey joke. She won't. No one deserves to have the place where they live mocked, not even her father. The mailboxes glow blue in a trick of dusk. The basalt smell of a neighbor's fireplace. A faraway seagull laments. Jo pulls the sides of her coat tighter and checks her messages. Lived.

Her assistant, calling about a cardiologist who forgot his conference ID.

Her assistant saying never mind, he found it.

Her assistant saying never mind the never mind, please call.

The last message is her mother's sister in California, apologizing for a change in plans that will prevent her from attending the funeral.

Jo slips the key into the lockbox, imagining the satisfying crack of opening a beer in her room at the Econo Lodge.

"I didn't like him but I wanted to come for you," her aunt says. "I appreciate that you have no siblings to help."

Jo hears a sound in her father's backyard and halts. Behind a green slatted gate, something animal stomps and haws.

"Your mother hoped you'd have a husband or boyfriend when the time came. Of course, she never imagined she'd go first."

Jo walks toward the yard as whatever lurks there quiets, detecting her. She hesitates before unlatching the gate. A motion light illuminates the driveway. She blinks to clear her vision, steadies herself against the flimsy tangle of plastic fencing.

On the other end of the line, her aunt sighs. "Kiddo, there is never a good time."

Jo opens the gate. The yard is half-bathed in synthetic light. Dark humps of mowing equipment, planters, and rakes abandoned near the back. A picnic table warped by years of weather relents against the earth.

In the center of the yard, on a patch of masticated grass, a silver unicorn stamps in place. Seeing Jo, it exhales sharply through its nostrils. Cold breath pillows above its head.

The motion light quits, plunging them into darkness. Jo loses her grip on the phone.

Back inside the house, Jo hunts the trash for the discarded zoo brochures. She calls the zookeeper and gets his voice mail. "Howdy," he says. "You've almost but not quite reached me." She hangs up, calls again and leaves a message. She repeats her phone number three times.

The unicorn has followed her. It hooves open the pantry door and pushes a box of matzo to the floor. The fulgid metallic hair that covers its body appears purple from certain angles, like the reed fields that turn and change color in wind. Its mouth is perfunctory and lopsided, and arranged—even when it's chewing steadily, like it is now—into a smirk. It does not seem violent or aggressive. It seems unenthused. If it weren't for the horn—the only pleasant thing about it, Jo thinks—navy-colored with flecks of glittery mineral issuing out from an active, spiraling core—it would look like a frustrated donkey.

Jo understands why it has been left in the backyard. It chews several crackers at once, leaving a mess. It gnaws the knob to the silverware drawer. She cannot leave it here to destroy the house. The unicorn follows her back into the yard. She re-latches the gate, leaving it inside. She walks to her car and turns the key in the ignition. Heat sighs through the vents. Jo resents the added responsibility this creature brings and the havoc it could wreak on her schedule. "Thanks, Dad," she says, to no one. Her voice sounds tried on, two sizes too big.

Jo drives to the strip mall where she finds the taco shop. Except for her father's orderly development, nothing in this town seems governed. Thin teenagers glare by the shop, curled like parentheses. Restless zoning restrictions permit a Kmart next to a real estate office next to an apartment complex. Jo cannot see the ocean but the ocean is everywhere: pooling in the swells between foxtails, frizzing the hair at her temples. Its mascot, the horseshoe crab, appears in decal form on car bumpers, motel signs. Seagulls holler over her as she walks back to the car. Anything left out in this night will be demoralized by cold and salt. She will not think about the creature standing alone, hunching its back against the wind, shifting its weight from hoof to hoof for warmth.

Her return to the yard summons the motion light. She peers through the gate slats to where the unicorn stands, regarding her, unsurprised.

Jo converts the back seat of her station wagon into what the manual calls an after-antiquing space. The unicorn climbs in and rests its chin on the console between the front seats.

"I can't drive with your head there," Jo says.

The unicorn snorts but doesn't move.

"It's a short ride," she bargains.

The unicorn repositions but leaves a rough hoof where it will brush against her hand when she shifts gears.

Jo and the unicorn drive to the Econo Lodge in silence. It spits when she attempts to help it unfold from the car. She leads it to her room, grateful that no one is in the reservation office or the pool decorated to look like a tropical island. Jo uses extra pillows and one of the motel's unfriendly blankets to hew a makeshift pallet. She fills the miniature coffee maker's carafe with water and places it on the floor. The unicorn sniffs but does not drink. Jo retrieves a bottle of apricot juice from her bag and refills the carafe. The unicorn laps it up. Jo refills it and the unicorn drains it again. Satiated, it flicks a critical gaze to the television, the bathroom, her clothes. It soundlessly swallows her hairbrush. Jo scrambles to zip her suitcase but the unicorn is too fast. It ingests a tube of mascara. Its tail twitches and an elegant line of feces plummets onto the thin carpet. The room fills with the tang of leather and armpit. The unicorn lowers itself onto the blanket and falls asleep.

Jo checks for balls and finds no balls. A girl, then. A feeling of solidarity shivers over her but is quickly replaced by the factual odor of dung. Jo turns on the television set. A newscaster named Jasmine reads tide reports for the Delaware Bay and Jo uses motel shampoo to scrub the feces out of the carpet. Jasmine, she thinks, a fragrant kind of rice.

Later, wet hair wrapped in a towel, Jo checks in with her assistant. The cardiologists are enjoying cocktail hour. They have complimented the ice sculpture she ordered to be cut in the shape of a heart.

Jo dials California and defines the term *cremains* for her aunt. She doesn't mention the unicorn farting in sleep, its flatulence sounding like the upper notes of a xylophone, operatically high. "Cremated and remains," she says. "A hybrid." The overspecificity feels like a gut punch. Hocked spit after your opponent is already down.

"And I will tell you what I told your father," the zookeeper says when he calls the next morning. "You are not equipped to take care of a creature of this nature."

Jo is driving and swatting the unicorn away from chewing the upholstery. "This morning it defecated on my suitcase."

"She," the zookeeper corrects her, "defecated on your suitcase."

Jo says, "I thought unicorns would be peaceful."

His laugh sounds like a mean bark. "You have a lot to learn about unicorns."

Jo crouches inside her father's bathtub, scrubbing grout. He was a retired electrician with no history of whimsy. What was he doing with a unicorn? Was it a gift meant to ease her grief? Was he holding it for someone who will show up to collect it—a wizard, or . . . ?

His bathroom is neat but not clean. It takes three tries to whiten the tub.

Jo returns to the living room, covered in bleach, and discovers that Jasmine has gnawed through one of the packing boxes filled with wrapping supplies. It has strewn ribbon and tissue paper across the carpet, making the space look like the aftermath of a party. She bats the unicorn's nose with an empty roll of ribbon.

"Bad Jasmine," she says.

———

That evening she meets the zookeeper at Applebee's. He is a squat man in high-waisted jean shorts with erratic facial hair. His speech is punctuated by the nervous, barking laugh. They sit in a padded booth and order dinner. It's been over two days since Jo has interacted with a live human being and she is giddy and talkative. She details the unicorn's eating habits and bad behavior. "Today, Jasmine kicked out the heating vent and broke the bathroom mirror."

"Jasmine?" The zookeeper chuckles. "That's a little girl's name. Her name is _____." He makes a sound like a breeze moving through plastic tubing in an open field.

He is part of a team working to repair beach erosion after a recent hurricane. Without enough sand, the horseshoe crabs won't have room to mate. This affects the red knot bird population arriving from Argentina expecting to refuel on crab eggs.

"Everyone here seems obsessed with horseshoe crabs," Jo says.

"They're as old as dinosaurs," he says. "Their relationship with the red knots is delicate and important."

Suspicion flicks over his face. Jo is aware he is drawing lines around himself and this town, but she's too tired to care about little birds.

"What is it you do, Jo?"

"I plan events."

He uses his fork to lift his steak as if he will toss it over the bank of booths. "You know how to make God laugh?"

"No," she says.

"You make a . . ."

She forks the last piece of chicken into her mouth and chews. She doesn't feel like participating in a joke about her work.

"Plan?" he says, finally.

In the lull between entrées and desserts, he hitches up his pant leg to reveal the silver slap of a gun. "I have one in my car too," he says.

Jo experiences simultaneous desires to laugh and run. "Who are you going to shoot at Applebee's?"

"No one, hopefully. But you'll be happy if we get robbed."

"If we get robbed?"

Mistaking her question for interest, he places the gun on the table for inspection.

"When are we getting robbed?" she says.

"I wouldn't know exactly, would I? Go ahead. Try the grip."

"No thanks." Like items into a purse, Jo gathers herself inside of herself.

"People get robbed here," he says. "We carry guns for protection. We care about the relationship we have to our surroundings. And the names we use matter. Your unicorn isn't an 'it,' she's a 'she.' Even your father understood that."

Jo realizes this man knew her father better than she did, and that her father has told him things about her. "Did you spend a lot of time with him?"

"I did." He leans against the hard plastic of the booth. "We were getting to be friends, maybe." He seems to be gauging whether she is ready to hear something. "He was a good man."

The waiter approaches, balancing apple cobbler on a tray. They look up from the gun on the table.

On the drive back to the Econo Lodge, Jo stops in to a liquor store. On a television hanging over the counter, the announcer named Jasmine reports on what she calls the ongoing horseshoe crab situation. The red knots are expected to land in a month. If the horseshoe crabs haven't produced enough eggs, the birds won't be able to gain enough sustenance to endure the second leg to Antarctica. They will fall out of the sky somewhere over Canada. A red knot appears on the screen. It is smaller than Jo would have guessed—the size of a Ping-Pong ball. "Even now, trucks from Texas are hauling tons of sand through the night," Jasmine reports. Jo imagines the zookeeper shooting bullets into a mound of sand.

At the motel, the unicorn is restless. She balks and pivots, drags her neck along the floor. Something red winks near her hindquarters. When Jo tries to investigate Jasmine figure-eights out of her grasp. Jo traps her in the bathroom between the sink and shower and looks closer. A few inches of ribbon hangs from the unicorn's sphincter. Wrapping ribbon from her father's house. That he used to wrap presents. For whom? She closes the door, trapping the whining unicorn in the bathroom. In the kitchenette, she pours whiskey into a glass and takes a long drink. The unicorn has ingested an unknown length of ribbon that now wants out. Jo could cut it but has no idea how much is left inside the creature.

She returns to the bathroom, closes the door, and kneels by Jasmine's side. She pulls the tail aside so it does not impede the opening and takes the ribbon between her thumb and forefinger. She tugs, revealing another half an inch. Anxiety flinches through the muscles of the unicorn's legs. Jo has never been this close to the creature. Her fur that looks bristly from afar is soft and parts easily to reveal improbably pink skin. A current of cool air circumnavigates her body—light-jacket weather. Jo pulls and the ribbon emerges slow inch by slow inch. Jasmine tenses, cries out. Jo slows her pace. The unicorn shudders as the end of the ribbon finally emerges. Jo flushes it and allows Jasmine to back out of the bathroom and sink into her makeshift bed. Jo dry heaves into the bathroom sink.

The next morning at her father's house, Jo finds a sleeve of Polaroids and, after initial hesitation, flips through them while sitting cross-legged on the floor. The bay at sunset. Two women, hips against his old LeSabre, rigid as coworkers. The girlfriend he left her mother for, wearing a sombrero. His parents smiling over eggs at the diner when everyone was still alive. Jo in a bank vestibule, brandishing a lollipop. Jo honking the LeSabre's horn. Leaping a sprinkler. Holding a turtle. Always alone. The sunset again, from a different vantage point. The sunset again. The sunset again. A tag of thumb at the corner of the photo. His thumb.

Jasmine rests on her father's bed, licking her hoof. When she's not chewing doorframes or urinating on Jo's clothes, the unicorn is good company.

"Look." Jo holds out the lollipop photograph. "This was me."

Jasmine climbs down and stretches her front legs. The bedspread is perforated by her rump, chin, and leg joints.

"He let you sleep with him?" Jo feels punctured, as if this would nullify an unacknowledged arrangement between her and her father, that he would stay isolated from other living creatures, as she had.

Family can slough away from you like bones shed meat in boiling water.

Jo's mother thought daughters and fathers should talk, no matter how unwilling the daughter, no matter how disputatious the father. After she died, there was no one to force them around a table. Their twice-annual phone calls ceased. Jo never called and he never called, afraid or unwilling to disturb the quiet that Jo convinced herself was peace. She didn't know he had been refusing dialysis for two years; they hadn't spoken in three.

At the Econo Lodge, Jo pauses over her crossword, filled with inexpressible relief. In the gentle, rented space, amidst the fwip of television, she realizes her father's death has canceled only his life. Their relationship, albeit one-sided, continues. When he was alive, there were times she forgot about him. Someone would mention his or her father, or the idea of fathers, and everyone would think of their own. Jo would wait the topic out, with no more emotion than one uses to write *not applicable* on a medical form. Existing conditions? History of diabetes? Father: NA. Then, something would catch and she'd realize, I have one of those. When he was alive, Jo never knew where her father was. Now his existence is irrefutable, his location exact and near: in incinerated fritters, sealed in the plastic depository on the coffee table, next to a box of matzo. Belief can create existence, but tonight the opposite is also true. For the first time, Jo believes in her father. This family is closer than ever.

Later, the zookeeper examines Jasmine then he and Jo share a six-pack.

"Pulling it out was the worst possible thing you could have done," he says about the ribbon. "It could have been tied up in her intestines."

"It wasn't." Jo is sulky, guilty. She finishes a beer and starts another.

"It's easy to mistake her size and attitude for strength." He sits on the edge of the bed next to her. "But there's a tranquility inside her that must be protected."

He takes her hand with surprising delicacy. Jo perceives a cue in his earnest, fixed gaze. She leans in and presses her lips against his. She answers what feels like hesitance with certainty. His hands hover but don't land on her body. She unbuttons her shirt and pushes his hand inside. Curled on a pile of blankets, Jasmine sighs, bored. Jo insists with her mouth though the zookeeper has no interest. Finally, he peels away from her grip and stands.

"Don't get upset but I'm going to go."

"Stay." Her blouse is open. Her bra is white and practically designed.

"Sometimes when we're grieving we think we want things we don't." It is obvious he is accustomed to talking unmanageable animals into things they're not interested in. She is not a wounded bird. She reaches for him again but he retreats.

His coat sags on a chair. She roots through it and pulls out his gun. It is a cold, dumb bar in her hand. She aims at his chest.

He raises his hands, smiling. "I give up."

She lets it fall to the bedspread with an innocuous thump. "Bang bang," she says.

He palms it and replaces it in his pocket.

"Did my dad ever . . ." Jo says. Every word she could use to finish the sentence leaves her mind. "Say . . ." she manages, ". . . anything?" She knows how pathetic she looks, unarmed on the bedspread.

"About you?" the zookeeper helps. "He said you were stubborn, like him." He looks as if he will reach out to her, thinks better of it, walks to the unicorn, nuzzles her ear, crosses to the door, and with a look in Jo's direction she can't decipher, leaves.

In her dream, an apricot asks Jo a series of difficult questions. She gets most of them right. Frustrated, the apricot lapses into a paroxysm of hooting.

Jo awakens, slick with sweat. The hooting has followed her out of the dream, transforming into a flute coming from the next room. Someone is practicing scales with the ambition of a newbie. That can't be, thinks Jo. Practicing an instrument is something one does in a permanent home. Motel rooms are for transitory activities like preparing for a meeting or dressing for a wedding. Do people live in the Econo Lodge? A breeze through the open door chills her. The open door that, Jo realizes, is open.

Jasmine is not in the parking lot or the motel store that sells car-specific items like replacement windshield wiper blades. Wearing pajamas and motorcycle boots, Jo runs through a copse of evergreens that connect the motel to a service road. She sprints the service road, streetlights switching on above her. Seagulls make erratic arcs over a figure in the distance. Teenagers jeer and throw cans. They've tied a rope around Jasmine's neck. They've fisted a newspaper into her mouth as a bridle. One of the boys mounts and sinks his heels into her hide. They close ranks. Jasmine blows and canters, attempting indifference. They kick out her back legs. The unicorn does not defend herself. She falls gracelessly against the asphalt.

"Hey," Jo yells.

One of the kids registers her with a quick slip of his tongue while another throws a broken bottle that pierces Jasmine's skin. Pain storms through the unicorn's body. Jasmine rolls her eyes toward Jo, who recognizes a familial sense of disappointment. Jo doesn't know how to put herself in between something she's responsible for and something that wishes to do it harm. Her people were withholders.

The unicorn lifts her head to the electric wires fretting above them and bays. The sound begins as the whine Jo has become familiar with but then it grows mythically, emergency loud. Jo covers her ears. The boys scrabble across the lot into a waiting truck and yell, "Go!" to the driver. The unicorn's cry grows louder, splintering the back windshield. The truck screeches away as its windows concuss.

Jasmine quiets. The lot is silent. Mackerel-colored bruises bloom along her shoulders. Blood pushes through the skin where the bottle hit; slippery and silver, like mercury. Jo rests her hand on Jasmine's neck. The unicorn shudders but doesn't protest. Halting occasionally so the unicorn can steel herself, they walk the service road back to the motel.

The expression of the Kmart cashier sours as she turns to the line and asks, "Who smells like horseshit?"

Jo holds a heating blanket, bandages, a jar of apricot juice, a tube of mascara, and a hairbrush. Jasmine waits in the car. "Me," she says.

Jo and Jasmine drive to the Econo Lodge in silence.

Jo cleans the unicorn's wounds and they watch television. Jasmine seems unfamiliar now. Seeing her in pain is like seeing someone in a bathing suit for the first time. So much exposed softness. Jasmine places her chin in the crook of Jo's elbow and heaves a relieved sigh. Jo is surprised by how much this intimacy pleases her. She runs her hands through the creature's silky fore-lock. She rests her head against Jasmine's and falls asleep.

On the last day, only the items in her father's bedroom closets remain. The first holds his casual clothes; sweaters folded and ar-ranged by color. Jo slides them into trash bags, relieved to be al-most finished.

Despite her best efforts, she has pieced together an image of her father's life: He lived on an impeccable cul-de-sac in an orga-nized house, eating diet dinners, shaving regularly, exercising his bi- and triceps with products ordered from television, and ignor-ing advice from doctors and zookeepers, with a drawer of old photos and a flatulent, possibly kosher unicorn. It was maybe not the most thrilling life but it was at least as happy as hers. She thinks of her second-floor apartment, the din of other people's children in the courtyard below.

The last closet holds his work clothes. Twenty or so replicas of the same evergreen jacket. Pockets for his tools. His name tag gleams on each left breast—she flips through them and it is as if her father is standing in front of her, repeating his name. Jo lifts as many coats as she can over the clothing rail. The collars press against her neck. The smell of his skin: cardboard and licorice. She inhales into the gruff fabric, his battered sleeves gathering her.

Jasmine's irritable nature, briefly anesthetized by pain, returns and, as if to make up for lost time, worsens. She takes proud dumps where it is hardest to clean, kicks through the door when Jo is in the shower. She belches and farts to fill the room with the odor of minty trash. She refuses to sleep, neighing and pacing by the foot of the bed until dawn.

After making the last of the funeral arrangements, Jo returns to the Econo Lodge to find that Jasmine has eaten most of the Polaroids. Those she has not subsumed she has mauled unrecognizable. The creature dozes in the corner, exhausted as Jo surveys the scene, mute with shock. She paces over the mutilated photos. A corner of sunset. Half of the Buick. She grips the unicorn's head unkindly. Jasmine tries to corkscrew out of Jo's hold but Jo is stronger. She screams into her face until the unicorn's cheeks quake and her eyes fill with pearly liquid. The unicorn cowers in the kitchenette. Jo hurls herself around the room until she collapses onto the skin-thin bedspread and dials the number by heart.

By the time the zookeeper arrives, Jasmine is attempting to repent. She nuzzles into Jo's side. She laps up her juice, taking care not to spill. When none of it works, she leans against the kitchenette, blinking and panicked. Jo sits on the bed, dismissing television channels. They both startle when he knocks.

Even though she called him, Jo glares through the peephole.

"It's cold out here," he says.

Jo opens the door and attempts aloofness. "How are the red knots? Has anyone heard from them?" He doesn't answer but makes the breeze-moving-through-plastic-tubing sound. Jasmine perks and trots toward him. Jo cannot anticipate the damage this act of recognition wreaks in her heart. Before she can protest, the zookeeper unfurls a gold leash and collar from his bag and secures it around the unicorn's neck. Jasmine nickers, flirting.

"What did you do to her forelock?" he says.

Jo feels accused. "I braided it."

He leads Jasmine out of the room to his truck. The unicorn follows his unapologetic gait, which annoys Jo, though she follows too, her breath coming in quick punches. "She's too much for me," she says, though she is suddenly not certain. A ramp extends from the flatbed and the unicorn back-walks into the kennel. "She doesn't have room to turn around."

"It's only ten minutes to the zoo." He snaps the door in place.

"I was wrong to think she could ever fit into my life. The other night she got out and kids attacked her." Jo knows she sounds desperate. She has failed her father in a way she doesn't understand. She wants the zookeeper to tell her she is making the right decision.

"Sounds like you could have used a gun." He starts the engine. "Look." His eyes stay trained on the roof of the Econo Lodge where a fistful of shorebirds gather to watch. "You did your best, but there was no way you could handle it. I told him that but he wouldn't listen."

The truck joggles across the lot. The unicorn stares whitely toward where Jo stands in the doorway. Under the slate sky, her metallic coat debates gray and purple, and appears to rise. The truck turns onto the service road. Jo waits until she can no longer see the wink of it through the trees. Until she forgets she is a person leaning against a doorframe, until she remembers, and is still unable to move.

———

At the funeral home, Jo places the cremains like a vase in the center of a platter of cold cuts. She and the executor sit on a mannered love seat and she signs the paperwork that concludes a life.

"Were you able to take a leave of absence from your job?" he says.

She is pleased he remembered. "I can work from anywhere. What I do doesn't require me to be present."

"And what is that?" he says.

Someone pushes through the front door. They look up in greeting but it is a churchgoer, mistaking the entrance. "I make God laugh," Jo says. She thinks he will look confused or get up and remix the dips stiffening in the parlor's stilted air. Instead, he smiles.

"That's what we all do."

No other mourner arrives. Jo and the executor wrap the cold cuts and seal the extra rolls in bags. He was a good man, the zookeeper had said. It's been bothering her for days.

"Can I ask you a question?"

"Yes," the executor says soberly.

"Would you call my father a good man?"

He pauses transferring cold cuts to a bag. "He always sent contracts back promptly."

The executor resists taking the leftover food, but accepts after Jo insists, voice breaking over the words. "Leftover food at my father's funeral."

"Can you think of a reason your father wanted you to have a unicorn?" he says. "He took wild risks to get it. Did you like them growing up? My girls love them. They have figurines, brush their hair, make waterfalls for them in the sink."

No doubt these are the girls who crafted the #1 DAD key

chain that hangs from his belt loop. Jo admits she's considered every possibility and has arrived at no conclusion. "Sometimes a unicorn is just a unicorn."

"You did the right thing, giving it to the zoo." He is already looking toward the parking lot where his car waits to take him home.

"She," Jo says.


Jo eats tacos and steers with her knees. She sits on the damp sand and watches the ocean hoist itself into the air. It is unapologetic and there are glints of anger in it and Jo appreciates this as she eats. She's alone. It's Sunday. Hundreds of miles south on another, warmer beach, one hundred cardiologists are being secured into life preservers. They will snorkel by the light of the moon then enjoy a champagne toast. Even with detours, the week has gone according to plan.

This ocean, however, is not one you can see the bottom of. Aggravation frills its waves. A hard-tailed horseshoe crab rudders through the sand and muck. One force pushes toward the shore while another pulls, clearing the previous wave's underlayer of silt. A seagull beats against calm air, arcing and holding, arc and hold, battling pressure only it feels.

But where are the red knots? Legs tucked into plumage sheared from struggle. Their gaze alert, expectant. Neutralizing their ache by communicating to one another in flight: a little more, a little more, a little more.

That morning Jo was charged a thousand dollars in room fees for the carpet, the mirror, the drapes, the vent, the shower curtain, the coffeepot.

The motel clerk rang her up with a pitiless look. "Rough night?"

Embarrassed, Jo had lied. "My sister can get a bit nuts."

Jo finishes her tacos and balls the wrapping. She would like to see a unicorn charge across the sand. Sister, she thinks, watching the shoaling waves.

The unicorn leaps from the brush and gallops across the field. Jo and the zookeeper watch her under the darkening sky. Her wounds have healed. Her coat shines. Jo realizes—how had she missed it?—that the creature advances and retreats in the same movement, obeying two instincts, the way her father would, even in the midst of his worst tirades, pause to drag his cheek against his shoulder, as if asking himself for pardon.

"You gave her to me," the zookeeper reminds her, "because you couldn't handle her."

"A decision I regret," Jo says. "However, my father left me everything he owned, and he owned her, so she is mine."

"She needs room to run." He gestures to the field. "Do you have a big apartment in New York?"

"I have a junior one bedroom," Jo says.

The nervous, barking chuckle. He points to the walking path where goldenrods flex in the cold breeze. "How about this? I'll go over there. We'll both call to her." 

This can't be how it's settled, Jo thinks. A simple call-and-response. But the zookeeper is already walking to his appointed spot. "If you know what's best for her, you shouldn't be worried."

Jasmine reclines in a thatch of foxtails, chewing the bulb of her heel. Darkness blots out the bordering trees, making the field seem endless. Somehow they both know he will go first.

"_____," he calls. A vestibule where chimes hang, a benevolent sound that mothers out background noise. For the first time since Jo entered this town, the scream of seagulls doesn't fill her ears. The unicorn looks up but doesn't move. He calls again. The unicorn rises and takes a few skittering steps. Jo envisions her drive home alone, mile markers flipping silently by. But Jasmine halts, investigates an infraction in the grass, and doesn't move again.

The zookeeper jockeys from foot to foot. He rattles his keys to get the creature's attention. He tries again, but Jo knows—it is no longer her name.

Jo stands in her appointed place, working up the correct voice. The air is so crisp it seems about to crack. Dusk hovers, carrying the threat of snow, but it's just another worry on the field. "She won't come to you either," the zookeeper assures her, but sounds uncertain. The unicorn reclines, unconcerned by the clash of wills being wrought over her name. Jo is battered by the desire to protect this heavy, unwilling thing and understands that this battering is love. She must allow it to do whatever it wants to her when she calls, "Jasmine, come to me."

# Can Only Houses
# Be Haunted?

Someone says, "Let's rent a farmhouse in the country.

"Let's pick peaches and swim, lie on blankets and read, make pies with the peaches we pick." They say country peaches are faultless. Even if you think you don't like them, once you've had one you can't imagine your life without them. So we load our sedan with what we know we're good at—bread recipes, Bananagrams—and what we hope we'll be good at—croquet, from a box of equipment we found *just lying on the street*. We spend the weekend in an after-the-second-drink malaise, swim laps, gorge on supple peaches, and with heavy mallets perform majestic roquets to make one another giggle. Each afternoon a breeze looses golden leaves upon our sunning bodies. The report of the screen door: Everything's fine. Everything rented. Lathered, reapplied. Watusi-ed. When Monday arrives, we idle in the kitchen, leftovers cellophaned, damp trunks drying on back windshields. It is the part of the afternoon when the light is most beautiful, and everyone feels slightly deceased.

That's when Riva and Aurelio mention they need a ride home.

My husband, Vig, hoists himself into a sitting position on the counter and says, "We'll take them," and I say, "But we were planning to stop into farm stands?" which is one of those questions that is really a statement, and instead of replying he asks Riva how she feels about farm stands, and of course she loves them because who doesn't?

The matter settled, we break ranks to run final checks of the bedrooms and hug Cooper, the farm's guileless, luminous retriever.

I fold towels and sulk. I'd been nursing an idea of myself strolling through aisles of produce, fingers bumping harmlessly over eggplants and cantaloupe. Riva is a clinging, anxious shopper who makes strolling impossible and I prefer shopping alone or with Vig, and Vig knows this. I didn't grow up with things like farm stands or croquet or whiskey glasses or even lawns. I'd borrowed money from my father to afford the weekend. Vig's offer to Riva violated a pact we have: No intruders. Us before everyone. We decline most invitations and sleep with weapons by our bedsides.

"Isn't this something we should have discussed?" I say, as we pull a macramé cover over the bed.

He passes me a glacial look. "Try to be friendlier."

Which hurts, of course, but I do it, I friendly up. I'm even smiling when we rejoin the group to discover that Riva and Aurelio forgot an errand they have on Frank's side of town, and it follows they should ride back with him. The problem is solved, yet as our sedan crunches down the driveway, the idea of our potential passengers shimmers as solidly as if they were safety-belted in the back: ghosts of some infraction Vig has committed against me.

Even Cooper's cheerful jowls as he gallops next to our car fail to please me. We may as well've taken the freeloaders home.

The bliss of the weekend already husking away from me, we pass the first farm stand. No longer interested but trapped by my earlier, forceful passion, I point and Vig dutifully pulls in.

Within moments we are standing in front of a stack of velvety peaches. In aggregate they seem to tremble with good health, but when I pick one up its tacky skin recoils from my touch, which figures. No one wants to be near me. "These are maybe not the ripest?"

"I'm sure they're fine," Vig says, though his gaze rests on a little boy, sitting in a shopping cart, gumming a banana peel. Seeing Vig, the boy chucks the peel onto the ground. His mother picks it up. The boy considers, chucks it again. Vig catches it and, smiling, returns it to the mother.

We bag eight peaches and join the line.

"If you'd like a kid," I say, "I'm happy to kick you in the shins." One of Vig's favorite things about me is my wit. I'm always saying things like Doing yoga is like lighting a candle and throwing it out the window. I have a running bit for children. Whenever we are doing something that would be rendered impossible by having them, I say, "Should we have children?" Cocktails at noon, cocaine at midnight, panting after one of our intense screws: Should we have children? I'm positive I am very funny.

"What a jerk," I prompt him, about the kid.

"Jerk," he says.

Driving out of the parking lot, we notice a parliament of gravestones near the highway entrance.

Vig announces: "This farm stand has been brought to you by the souls of your dead relatives."

This brightens my mood. I'm thinking, If he's willing to make a silly remark, maybe this ride can be salvaged.

During our first years together, we offered each other copious tangible examples of our love. A vintage pencil sharpener, the kind you crank. New ways to make a hamburger. This grew tiring. Eventually, humanely, we allowed each other rest from being impressive, which was comforting until it became uneasy, something we weren't sure we'd invited.

That night, a clattering in the kitchen wakes us. Metal against metal, a collision of separate things against a solid. In the rubbed nothing of predawn Vig and I wait to see if it is a solitary disturbance, able to be explained by a surprise of wind through our measly screens, or whether it will prove itself malignant by repeating. Wind, I pray.

Another burst of noise.

Vig sleeves the crowbar he keeps on his side of the bed, and I take hold of the bat I keep on mine. Armed, we creep down the hallway and stall in fear when we reach the kitchen. Whatever is behind the door overturns a drawer of silverware.

Vig straightens, his mouth in a serious line. Giving himself a pep talk in the voice of his sixth-grade baseball coach, no doubt, the one who gave him the chance to bat during the only game his mother attended. I know every inflection of that story better than I know certain friends. He told it two days before while everyone treaded water in the swimming hole, feet pale disks pedaling beneath us.

Strike one. Turn and face his mother. Strike two. His mother digging for something in her purse. Full count, etc. . . .

Vig traces a square in the air, points downward, points to me, the square again. I get that he wants me to stay behind him while he opens the door, but Vig doesn't trust my ability to understand simple facts. He hisses, "Stay behind me while I open the door." He turns the knob and soundlessly pushes.

In the corner of our kitchen, an eyeless girl carangs the

emptied silverware drawer against the antique hutch I bought when I was single. Cutlery is piled in jagged hills by her ankles. She's seven or eight. But also a million? It's obvious she's been dead for a while, even to Vig, who usually requires three unrelated sources to believe anything. Gray skin corkscrews off her throat. Exposed veins reach toward the overhead light. A glowing current throbs around her, tethering her to the fruit bowl, where the peaches we bought seize and pitch. They are attendant in this haunting, each one pulsing with a force that wants out. We both realize this simultaneously, still Vig whisper-screams, "She came from the peaches."

"Vig. I know!"

The dead girl swivels at the sound of our voices. She produces the steak knife I'd asked Vig to sharpen but now I'm glad he never did because she hurls it at us then reloads with a soup ladle.

We retreat into the hallway and slam the door. I suck in air and Vig paces.

The dead girl is still throwing cutlery, and now it sounds like she's crying. Sloppy-sounding and exact. *Boo hoo*, she says. *Boo hoooooo.*

"She's crying," Vig says needlessly. "What do you think she wants? With us, I mean."

"I don't know what she wants," my tone meant to remind him that it doesn't matter what she wants.

Her boo hoos intensify.

Vig's expression digs at me. The way he looked at the dead girl was the same way he looked at the farm stand kid, a mixture of wonder and longing. "Do you think she's trying to find her mother?"

There is no doubt this jab is deliberate. "Maybe her mother is working," I say.

"This is not about you," Vig says. Which makes me certain it is.

*Boo hoo*, says the dead girl. An antic, performative sound. Perhaps she's only heard of human sorrow?

Vig rests his hand against the doorjamb, as if to console the girl. "She's more scared of us than we are of her." It's a personal reflection; he's given up speaking to me.

"I knew this would happen," I say.

"You knew a dead girl was going to rise from the produce?"

"Something felt off. My nerves have been—"

"Your nerves." The word returns us to an argument we'd had at the farmhouse. My nerves are famous within our relationship and were the reason I'd given when I suggested we wake everyone up early in the morning.

"Frank would've slept until midnight!" I hiss. "I didn't want to miss the day!"

"Did you think we were going to say good night and never see each other again?"

The discomfort of the weekend's conclusion settles over me newly, how quickly Vig offered a place in our car even though he knew I wanted to drive home alone, open to whatever sprang up along the way that seemed doable. Even though I couldn't articulate what those doable activities might be, I wanted him to protect my desire to do them. Refueled, my anger catches onto itself and spreads.

On the other side of the door, the dead girl drags what sounds like the table across the floor. Walnut, a vintage find. I imagine the divots she is carving into the hardwood floor.

"What if there are more?" Vig says. "We bought eight."

We realize that we've each ingested a peach and look down at our stomachs, expecting mutiny. None comes. In a moment I can only describe as relationship telepathy, we understand how we can get rid of her. Vig explains it anyway.

"If she came from the peaches"—he points to the kitchen—"and we eat the rest of the peaches—"

"I know, Vig!"

"I can't re-kill that dead girl," he says at the same time as I say, "I'll hold her down."

"Are you empathizing with something that just threw a steak knife at us?"

"Listen to her," he says. "She's sad."

"She's dead!"

"So judgmental!"

"Not a judgment. Not up for debate. She's fucking dead."

"Still. She's a—"

"Don't say it."

". . . guest in our home."

"A pest! A roach or one of those box insects that crawl into the air conditioner."

"Stink bugs," he says. "Don't even bite."

"This is my house. That's my steak knife. You're on her side!"

"A little girl!"

"An intruder!"

Our arguments tend to hedge between hurtful and comic. I'm wondering which side we're on when another knife hits the door and sticks. Vig shakes his hesitance. "You're right," he says. "Let's get her."

I preen in this rare give. It's my turn to pantomime. I point to the kitchen, pretend to hold a struggling thing, point to him, pretend to quickly eat a number of ball-shaped things.

We reenter the kitchen. The dead girl cries cruddy tears in the corner, clutching one of Vig's childhood spoons. A bunny-shaped handle.

It's always the singular first-person pronoun with him, I think as we creep toward her. Always, I can't re-kill the dead girl, never we.

"I'm sorry," Vig says. "Maybe you can find another home where people are better equipped to handle you?"

Her soulless gaze darts around the room. My shadow stripes her when we approach, yet she fixes on Vig. She senses he is the more emotionally permeable, her veins plead for him, as if I'm not capable of maternity. Her whole body palpitates as she weeps. I make myself as wide as possible and trap her while Vig clamps on to the furred flesh of the first peach. He bites down and the dead girl reacts as if punched. Even before swallowing the first he takes another, bigger bite. Juice streams down his chin and pools in the hollow between his collarbones. He bites again and again, the pulp of the pulp, finishing it.

"Watch the hardwood," I remind him, attempting to make my voice jaunty.

He looks at me with lifeless eyes.

The dead girl throws herself at me, her decomposing body like sandpaper against my bare arms. Burns bloom where she touches me.

"Are you seeing this?" I say, but Vig has turned toward the hallway, unable to watch her suffer. This ignites something unprocessed in me. Now the dead girl and I are both yowling. With every bite, her pain increases. Burns bloom where she touches me. My throat convulses as vomit ascends.

Two peaches remain. We're going to make it. Vig chews through a choking fit that slows his progress. I yell for him to hurry and he tells me to for once in my life be goddamned patient. One peach to go. Vig runs his bottom molars across the soft meat as if it were a corncob. He finishes. With a teeth-shattering shriek, an arc against the sky, the girl's outline advances its grotesque theory, quibbles, then fades.

She's gone. What's left are the pits. Flinty-looking with clots of jam and marrow. "We have to get rid of them too," I say. "Can't take chances."

"It's over," he says. "You got what you wanted."

I've been told I've a tendency to grow inches taller with indignation. I tower over him. "What I?" I show him the burns on my arms. "She tried to kill me! Someone needed to do something."

He says, "Don't say it."

"What kind of man—"

"There it is," he says. "Set your watch. It always ends with the man thing. Honestly, honey? You need a new act. I am the man I am. Able to show love the only way I know how."

"Show love?" I soil the word. "Where love? What love? Sounds nice. I'd like to order some of that."

He disappears through the back door. This is it, I think. The final final, but he returns carrying a croquet mallet. He raises it over his head and sends it down on one of the pits, which splinters under the assault. "This is love!" He brings the mallet down again, obliterating another oaky center. His aggravation has faded into mania. He's giddy, irreverent. "My love! For you!" The mallet comes down, catching the morning light eking through the windows. "This is my devotion!" The mallet comes down, bruising the hardwood. "My manhood!" His absurdity has surpassed mine. He's won.

I laugh, in spite of myself. Surprised, he turns to me. His posture softens. He hoists the mallet to the opposite shoulder, so I will laugh again.

"Do you like this?" he says. I say, "I do."

He thrusts his hip to the side, bats his lashes. "And this?"

I say, "Very much."

Of course, it was already over. It had been since Vig leaped to a sitting position on the rented counter and offered Riva and Aurelio a ride.

Before the country weekend, all of it—us, I mean, Vig and me—had been beginning to end—the initial descent. We lingered in the doorway between stopping or saving. Neither of us knew how to kick the relationship toward the good side or, more likely, neither of us knew which side was good.

I hated the way he said "ice cold milk." Worse than double homicide, that sound. Every night it seemed he wanted a glass of it.

"You know what I could go for?" he'd say, as if he didn't posit the same thing every night. "A glass of ice. Cold. Milk."

You should like the way your partner says milk. But I know less than nothing. For example, I don't even remember one way to make a hamburger.

I hadn't thought about that dead girl for ages until yesterday when someone asked if only houses can be haunted. And Tessa

said, "Yes, only houses and buildings." This was after the morning meeting, when we usually loiter in the conference room de-
ciding whether to eat the other half of the bagel. Tessa is always
correcting me over things that mean nothing, over things that
aren't even things. She reminds me of Vig.

I hadn't thought about Vig in a while either, but now he's as
present as if he were sitting at the conference table with us, slath-
ering jam onto a scone. The truth is, I can't remember him ever
saying he didn't want children. All deception is self-deception.
They don't tell you that in lying school. How disappointed he
must have been with me, a girl who wouldn't give her friends a
ride home. How unlike a country peach I am. How filled with
flaw. I hope whoever he's with now grew up with enough of
everything so they never feel the need to hoard.

So I told my office mates that I once fought a dead girl who
came from a haunted bag of peaches and their expressions
switched to *tell us more*. Which is a welcome change from how
they normally look at me, a combination of *who let that fly in* and
*this paint color is darker than it seemed on the chip*. I haven't been
working this job or living in this town long, and I realized the
story might curry me friendship. I'm not above using personal
low points as currency. So I told them about the dead girl and the
peaches and they asked questions until it would have been decep-
tive not to mention it had happened with an ex-husband.

"That was the last experience we had together," I said. "Unless
you count divorce."

Thinking about it now, however, divorce is more procedure
than experience. A removal that produces a scar. One thing gone,
one added. Something moves on, something remains. Which is
why anything can be haunted as long as there is residual memory

and a location, and a location can be a seashore, a truck cab, a body, a peach. So I agree with my first statement. It was the last experience Vig and I had together, in the part of a relationship when you agree without consult to avoid opening the door for the thing that will unravel you. How interested we are in delaying the inevitable when the inevitable has never been anything other than the most patient, caring lover on earth.

# Lottie Woodside
## and the
## Diamond Dust Cher

○

Lottie Woodside was learning—it takes two fools to start a marriage and a team to end one. Lawyers, a notary clerk, Derek even brought the girlfriend: an overmatched but dear-looking thing who avoided Lottie's eyes and sat on the bench in the notary's hallway, reinforcing her bangs with a purse comb.

"I hope you promised her ice cream after," Lottie said, and immediately regretted it.

Since they had agreed to divorce, Derek preferred to keep their interactions brisk and professional, but the finality of paperwork and a state building seemed to stir old compassion. "Well, you know," he said. Lottie knew this phrase, unfinished and delivered with chagrin, was meant to be conciliatory, a hand up into her new life.

The marriage was defunct. Thirty years folded into a drawer like holiday linens.

Lottie thought this earned her a cab ride.

She found one but upon opening the door saw that it was already occupied by a woman who, talking on her phone, blinked into the surprise of a new person. Lottie scanned the street for another cab but the woman waved come in, as if her departure would be more of a delay.

"I might not be on the way," Lottie said.

"Everything is on the way," the woman said. Then, into her phone: "Not you, Steve. The woman getting into this cab." The cabdriver protested but the woman seemed to be in control of his cab and everyone in it.

The light turned green.

Lottie gave the cabdriver her Brooklyn address.

The woman caught her looking at the large, flat package wrapped in brown paper and propped against her knees. Her hand flew instinctively to protect it. Whoever was on the end of the line expressed dissatisfaction. "Relax," the woman whispered. Lottie pretended not to notice the woman scanning her. "She's no dealer. Sandals with socks."

Lottie pressed her forehead against the cold window. She had taken a personal day from her nannying job and was looking forward to getting home. She planned to scrub Derek from their apartment with cleaning supplies that smelled like trees and by moving the couch from one side of the room to the other.

At a red light, the cabbie consulted the women in his rearview mirror. "We're going nowhere fast."

The woman leaned in to the partition separating them. "Can you try Tenth?" Elegant cuff links blinked on one sleeve.

The cab driver pulled out of traffic and performed a quick turn. The street was clear. He reached Tenth Avenue and made a sharp left, jostling the women against each other.

"Pardon me," said Lottie.

Yards ahead, a streetlight turned yellow. The cabdriver accelerated.

Lottie pointed to a spot on the floor near the package. "You lost one of your cuff links."

"Did I?" The woman clutched at her sleeve. "Hang on, Steve." She bent over the package to feel around on the floor. "These things never stay where they're supposed—"

Lottie didn't hear the rest of the sentence. She was outside the cab, sitting on the curb, legs arranged uncomfortably beneath her. An expression of glass fell over her in waves. A gem shone on the pavement. It turned and signaled to someone. To her? Lottie leaned in; her eyes adjusted and the object resolved into focus. The woman's cuff link. Lottie's handbag slumped against a nearby hydrant. She stood, shook her arms and legs. Her backside ached. Where the curb stopped me, she reasoned.

A Subaru had collided into the cab on its left side, where the woman had been searching the floor. Its driver was out of his car holding his head, wondering at the wreck. The cab was pummeled into a crescent shape; the cabbie settled on one side of it, the woman on the other. Lottie saw where her door had flown open and ejected her. The cabdriver's cheek rested against the steering wheel, smiling dimly in a good dream. Lottie had been in the presence of death only once and it was unmistakable.

In the back seat the woman clutched at her chest, as if trying to locate the pendant to a necklace. The cab steamed and bitched around her. "I'm okay," she said.

People clambered out of the surrounding shops, wanting jobs. They asked who needed assistance and made phone calls. Lottie picked up her handbag and shook it. How lucky, she thought, everything that belongs to me is intact. In the distance, a siren yearned toward them. The woman in the back seat cried for help. Her door was stuck. Strangers took turns pulling. The ambulance arrived. Paramedics spilled out and tended to the drivers, the woman. A policeman established a divide with yellow tape, creating a temporary order that Lottie appreciated. No one not directly involved in the accident should be allowed to participate.

Someone identified Lottie as involved in the crash, and a paramedic slipped an oxygen mask over her mouth and nose. She sat on the curb breathing into it while the others worked on the cabbie. She was certain he was dead so when his eyelids rebooted, when he exited the cab unassisted, Lottie felt some cousin of duped. It felt stranger than anything else that had happened: man returned from the dead. The crowd watched him attempt tentative, directionless steps. He made it to the corner and threw up into a city trash can. The paramedics turned to the woman in the back seat who'd gone quiet.

It was the kind of overfamiliarity that Harolyn had hated, but Lottie liked that the doctor used *we* and *us*, as if they'd both been in a wreck.

"Are we married?" he said, placing against her breastbone a stethoscope he'd breathed onto twice to warm. There are two kinds of doctors: those who warm the stethoscope and those who don't.

For the first time in thirty years, Lottie answered the question in the negative. We are not married.

"Is there anyone we should call?"

She pictured Harolyn the last time she saw her, laughing at a family of picnickers battling the wind on Higbee Beach. She felt the familiar, happy pain of missing her friend.

He shone a light into her eyes. "What is today's date?"

"I never know the date," Lottie said.

In a framed picture on the shelf behind him, the doctor was smiling the same way he was smiling now, his arm around a blond man holding a SOLD! sign.

"It's Memorial Day," he said. "The start of the summer. What's the last thing we remember?"

Lottie told him she'd hailed a cab that had been hit by another car. The police had driven her there, to the Midtown hospital, over her insistence. Now she was talking to him. She wasn't nauseated, had no neck or back pain, had no trouble breathing.

"You'll be sore tomorrow," he assured her, penciling a prescription for painkillers. "If you're feeling signs of a concussion, come back. Sometimes these things hit us later. Confusion. Forlornness. Scattered thoughts. Mania. Euphoria. It signals swelling of the brain. You think you're fine, then boom!"

"I'm seventy," Lottie said. "What you're describing is Wednesday."

She asked how the driver made out and he told her fine.

"And the woman?"

The doctor blinked several times. "I'm sorry."

So the one she thought would make it didn't, and the one she thought wouldn't did. "I didn't know her." Though appropriate, the sentiment fell short. Something about nearness, fondness, something about significance acting out of proportion with time. A nurse's arrival seemed to signal to the doctor that their visit had concluded. "That's a lot to process," he said. "Stay if you need a minute." When he was a child, he must have been every teacher's favorite. His pinched, sincere expression reminded her of Pumpkin, the little boy she nannied. "Don't forget your things." He pointed to her purse and a package propped against the wall. Lottie recognized it as the one from the cab.

"That's not mine," Lottie said. But the doctor and nurse were gone.

It was hard to believe she and the package had emerged from

the same car. Its wrapping was intact. Its pristine label indicated an office on the Upper East Side. Lottie carried it out of the hospital.

Lottie found a nearby coffee shop and ordered a sandwich and a cup of tea. At a free table she propped the package up on its own chair. She tugged at the tape and gently pulled down the wrapping to reveal a brightly colored portrait of Cher.

"Tuna salad!" the barista called.

Lottie left the painting to retrieve her order. At the condiment stand she shook pepper onto the bread, a habit Derek hated. She used more than she normally would, chewed, and studied the painting. Cher wore a sheer crocheted halter and sat elegantly slumped. She smiled with her mouth closed, lips outlined twice in black, eyes bright. Lottie returned the woman's heavy-lidded smile, enjoying the feel of the sun through the window flattening against her collarbones. Someone had said it was the beginning of summer. It sure was. Ambulances seared past the coffee shop, no doubt heading for the scene of her accident. No, that would have been cleared already.

Lottie finished her sandwich and reclothed Cher. The address on the label was up twenty streets and over three avenues. She walked to the bus stop, pausing to wait out a surge of pain in her lower back.

An almost-empty bus arrived. Lottie and Cher had their own seat. Schools were letting out; at every stop, children charged onto the bus, yelling and draping themselves over her seat with no apology, until Lottie had to balance Cher on her lap. Lottie never minded children as Derek had. She liked that they made split-second judgments and that they looked her in the eye. Most of the time Lottie enjoyed the invisibility that came with being older, the fact that no one thought she was capable of anything criminal or notable, but on this day she wanted to be seen.

At each stop children hurled themselves down the stairs, into the arms of parents and nannies and by the time they reached the Upper East Side, a neighborhood of art dealers and museums, the bus was empty again. Lottie and Cher disembarked and walked to the address, where Lottie repeated her name into the intercom.

"Who are you here to see?" The receptionist sounded doubtful. "We're booked."

"Steve?" Lottie tried.

The door buzzed and Lottie opened it. She climbed four flights to a gallery space where a young woman sitting at a small, gleaming desk greeted her.

"Is this about the Basquiat?"

"I was in a car accident," Lottie began, but then a man yelling from an office on the other side of the space startled the receptionist. The girl gestured to a folding chair next to a stack of magazines, crossed the room, and disappeared behind the door.

"Is it her?" the man said. "It's been hours."

"It's an old lady," Lottie heard her say.

Lottie gave Cher the chair and looked at the art. On an overlarge canvas the word RAPE stood against a field of crudely sketched penises.

"Isn't it amazing?" The girl stood behind her. "The artist is a public defender of rapists." She gestured across the space. "Over there will be our Warhol exhibit. All the diamond dusts arrive today. That's why it's a zoo."

Lottie let out a low whistle. "Diamond dust," she said.

From the office Lottie heard the sound of something large being thrown against metal. The man yelled for the girl, who jogged to rejoin him. They did not keep their voices low. "It's only been a few hours. You know her, she's probably talking. There's a woman here to see you."

"What does she want?"

"I haven't asked yet."

"If it's not your job to ask her, whose is it?"

Lottie remembered what it was like to work in an office like this. She remembered refreshing her makeup after crying in the bathroom. Bonding with people her age. She'd met Harolyn when they worked on the same floor of a Midtown building. They ate their sandwiches out of wax paper, sitting on the same park bench every day. Lottie thought she'd spend the rest of her life meeting Harolyn at twelve forty-five. But Derek disrupted her schedule, slightly, then more. She couldn't remember when or why she'd left that job. She couldn't even remember the building's address. And she spent so many years there.

A phone rang in the back office. The man said, "It's me."

The receptionist emerged. "It's not a good day," she said. "He won't be seeing clients."

"I'm not a client," Lottie reminded her.

"Oh my god," the man yelled. "Anna!"

"That's me," the girl said.

Lottie nodded. She had made a decision. "Good luck with the diamond dusts."

"Diamonds aren't even rare. Everyone thinks they are but they're not." Her voice was sorrowful. "Did you want to leave a message? I can take down your name." But the girl was already turning to the back office where he was calling her again. "No need." Lottie picked up the painting and started toward the door. She stepped into the vestibule and pressed the button for the elevator, which came at once. As the door closed, she heard the man's hot voice and the receptionist's salving replies.

"She wasn't a client. In a car accident. Sandals and socks."

"Well, bring her in!"

"Well, she's gone!"

In the lobby, men argued over a pallet of boxes. Lottie maneuvered past, through the door to the street. She was relieved to hear an enormous lock activate behind her.


Lottie wasn't certain what she was doing was stealing, but she wasn't certain it wasn't. She'd bring the painting back after she had time to think. The bus was nearing Midtown when her cell phone rang.

It was her employer, Alice Blakeman, who about the birth of her son, Pumpkin, once said: "I would have been just as happy had we adopted a cocker spaniel."

"I know it's your day off," Alice said. "But just for an hour?"

Lottie wanted to go home, take off her shoes, and scrub the walls. But she needed hours. Though guilt had made Derek financially considerate, the divorce had been expensive. She and Cher disembarked at the next stop.

Lottie and Cher crossing Fifty-Sixth Street.

Lottie pulling Cher away from a delivery cart's path.

Lottie and Cher waiting for a walk sign next to a pharmacy

window that seemed to reflect all the light in the world. Amidst the blurred, bright people crossing and waiting, Lottie was a hunched figure in a light jacket. She thought of Cher's certain gaze and straightened herself.

Lottie and Cher weaving through commuters belching up through the Fifty-Ninth Street subway exit.

In the Blakeman office, Pumpkin jumped on the couch while Alice stood on a chair in the center of the room, spraying him with water.

"Thank god," Alice said when Lottie entered. She motioned to Pumpkin with her shoe. "Ice cream, or whatever?"

Lottie and Pumpkin walked to the ice creamery on Fifth. Pumpkin ordered three scoops of mint julep. Lottie ordered one scoop of vanilla.

"Why would you order one scoop when you could have three?" Pumpkin said.

They sat on a low stone wall that bordered a park. Families dotted the lawn. Pumpkin stabbed at his ice cream with his small, pink tongue. Lottie had once attended Derek's company picnic in this park. They had crossed this lawn holding eggs balanced on spoons. Teams. On the subway home, Derek had said he was proud of his "jock wife." He balanced a platter of macaroni salad sheathed in plastic wrap on his thighs.

The sun retreated behind a cloud and threw shadows onto the field. The boy sitting next to her dragged his tongue across his ice cream while turning the cone for advantageous angles. He was attached to her, this was clear by how close he sat, how relaxed he was in her presence. Who was he?

"Do you like your ice cream?" she said.

He nodded. "It's delightful."

It was Pumpkin, she realized. The wealthy boy she cared for, who every so often opened into a moment of startling tenderness. Lottie worried these moments would become rarer as he aged. What did Harolyn always say about life? It's like a piece of pottery. A kite? A bike. "Was I here yesterday?" Lottie said. "Did I watch you?"

Pumpkin nodded. "We made turkey casserole for Alice."

"You're a good boy," Lottie said.

"What is that?" He pointed to the package.

Lottie unwrapped the top half of the painting, revealing Cher from the chin up.

"Ugly," Pumpkin said.

Lottie felt a stab of loyalty. "It's modern art."

Pumpkin produced a marker from his pocket and, before Lottie could stop him, drew a pert mustache on the canvas. She slapped his hand, sending the marker through the air to clack against the concrete.

"Ouch," he said, more loudly than the slap warranted. Receiving no response, he said it again.

"I want to know," Lottie said, "what made you think you could do that."

He retreated, flashed, hardened into a plan. "I'm telling Mother."

She licked her fingers and tried to erase the smudge. It blurred and spread. She pulled Pumpkin off the bench, to the curb, across the street, toward his mother's office.

———

Lottie and Cher sitting on the bus.

"No, thank you," Lottie said, when a man offered his hand.

Lottie and Cher leaping to the sidewalk.

Shop owners hosed off hot concrete. It was the beginning of summer. Or summer was almost over. In any case, the sun was to be enjoyed, because it had been absent for so long or because it would soon be going away. It was dusk when Lottie and Cher walked home through the park. The lamps were lit. Baseball games were concluding in the fields. Winners and weepers. Reluctant families trudged toward the subway.

Her apartment had three rooms: bedroom, kitchen, and family. Pale yellow walls and a partial view of the park, if you hung out the window upside down like a bat, clenching the railing with your toes. This was her joke with Pumpkin, and it never failed to elicit his throaty, adult laugh.

Lottie sat on the couch, removed her shoes, and spent a long time rubbing each foot. Her ancient answering machine flashed with a message. The gallery, she assumed, but it was Alice Blakeman.

"I don't know what to say. Pumpkin tells me—it's hard to even believe—he says, well, Lottie, did you slap him?"

This would be the most thought Alice would ever give her and it would come in the form of bewilderment that someone on her payroll would do anything to confuse her. Lottie knew that over the course of the night the confusion would calcify into self-righteousness, then insult. Lottie would have to apologize.

"Or else what?" she said aloud, rubbing and making a difference to a knot in her heel.

Across from the couch, a painting of an Italian café hung over the dusty television. "A conversation starter," Derek had called it.

He'd bought it during his traveling phase when he read about other countries and went nowhere.

It was meant to be their starter apartment, but they had lived in it for thirty years until a few weeks before, when Derek came home from his job at a medical supply firm and told her he would be moving into his girlfriend's apartment that very night. She was a coworker and had attended the park party, watching the couple cross the lawn holding eggs on spoons. She'd even expressed regret that no one had eaten Lottie's macaroni salad. "A waste of good noodles."

Though it had been Derek's decision to divorce, they'd both participated in the relationship's dimming. His dalliances, her aloofness. There were no children or money to divvy. There had been a baby who hadn't lived long. When Lottie pictured her, which she'd been doing more often, she lay in the hospital's bassinet on one of her only days, too delicate for the world to hold. The only time she'd been in the presence of death before that morning's accident. Weeks of damaging silence followed. Derek couldn't meet Lottie's gaze. He never blamed her but did not contradict her when she blamed herself.

Lottie poured a glass of wine and waited for remorse to split her in two. Garden-variety doubt, at least. No feeling arrived. Even after a second glass. She liked that the dishes in the sink were hers. Her work dresses, pressed and zipped, hung in the front closet. A headache bloomed at the base of her neck. She thought of Derek in this space as she throated two aspirin. He'd always looked too big in it, clumsy fingers pulling a pot from a high shelf.

Lottie removed Cher from her wrapping and leaned her against the wall. Except for Pumpkin's smudge, Cher was flawless, making everything in the room seem dull. Her patient, beaming face. The bold lavender and fuchsia. They smiled at one another.

Lottie propped Cher on one of the kitchen chairs, turned on the radio, and pulled a pork cutlet from the refrigerator. She liked noise while she made dinner. On the news, a man was being interviewed about something that had nothing to do with Lottie or anyone she knew. She chopped chives as the water boiled, tossed a pad of butter into a warming pan.

Lottie and Cher eating dinner at the kitchen table.

Lottie had never felt young, not even in youth. She disliked only one thing about time: the accrual of loss. At fifty, Harolyn said, people start to leave the room. Sometimes Lottie would shop to take her mind off all the good people gone. Harolyn, her baby, several dear friends, Derek too, in a way. She'd miss parts of him. The evil you know, Harolyn would say. Harolyn had been the most person with a capital *P* Lottie had ever known. No one made her do anything. How had death managed it? One moment you're a person and the next you're not.

After dinner, Lottie surveyed the family room. A knobby couch, an easy chair, two bookcases. She removed the café picture and replaced it with Cher. She stepped back and studied the woman.

"This must seem so shabby to you."

Lottie ran the vacuum over the family room and hallway carpets. The couch was lighter than she had anticipated. Or she was stronger. She dragged it to the opposite wall. The easy chair to where the couch had been. The television to the other wall. This rearrangement would create an enclave for Cher, she thought as she yanked the plug from the socket, a sacred space. She walked to the kitchen and retrieved a pint of ice cream from the freezer.

It occurred to her that the enclave should be on the smaller wall. The far wall did not offer the type of intimacy an enclave required. Lottie dragged the chair back across the room to the smaller wall, but there it was too close to the couch. The room creaked to one side, Cher in the middle, a steady rudder. Lottie pushed the couch to the far wall. Now the television was next to the couch instead of across from it. Then the bookshelves: two five-tiered towers of unfinished wood that Derek had put together with nails and a high heel. He wasn't all bad. It's impossible to hate a person you truly know.

Lottie decided to move the couch to the bookshelf wall and the bookshelves to the green wall, creating the enclave she desired. She had to progress inch by inch. First one bookshelf, then the next, then she ran to the couch and moved it a few inches. Lottie realized too late that the couch wouldn't fit past the bookshelves. She should have done one bookshelf then the other. She tried to move the chair to make way for the bookshelves. It lodged between the couch and the wall and refused to budge.

Lottie's strength was gone, her hands chapped and red. She attempted to lift the television over the couch to free up some space, but it was too stubborn to move. Lottie had positioned each piece of furniture so it could move neither forward nor back. A miracle of geometry.

Her headache was not responding to the aspirin, and an hour had passed. Or, three. Why the headache? It had been a regular day. She'd looked after Pumpkin and picked up a sleeve of veal on the way home for dinner. No, that was the year before. It had been Derek who knew what to do with veal. He'd surprised her with dinner and a fistful of wildflowers. They'd eaten at the kitchen table as the room filled with afternoon sunlight. If that was the previous year, what was today? Lottie remembered the accident, the painting. The lamp on the table next to her was off. She must have done it in her sleep. Her heart thumped. Had it been a dream, the cab, the Cher? No! There she was on the wall, every part of her glimmering in errant light. Two women in a room. Both survivors of a recent wreck.

"We've experienced quite a shock," Lottie told her. It was the right sentiment: honest, simple. A kiln, Lottie remembered. Is what Harolyn said life is like. It turns up the heat until your true colors show.

# The Ecstasy
of Sam Malone

◯

The year I gave college a try, one of the only professors I liked talked for what felt like forever about the false self. The part of one's personality ruled by insecurity, scarcity, and vice. The false self loves a party, he said. The false self loves to talk. I remember these lectures—some of the only I attended—as if I were still in that sunken brown classroom, listening to laughter on the quad and longing for escape. This was before I started doing things on purpose, a time that professor would probably refer to as when the false self drove. I was still a barfly and did not connect my malfeasance to anyone else's pain. I'm not proud of anything that happened the night it changed, which began, innocuously enough, when I drive to my mother's house to steal.

It is the feast of Saint Mary Magdalene de'Pazzi and there are figurines of the bewildered-looking nun tucked behind gate-posts, mailboxes, stoops. When my friends and I reach my mother's house, her mussed hair and the pressed map of fabric on her face makes it clear she'd fallen asleep. Yet she ushers us in, asking do we want coffee? Piece of pie? Tea? She has decaf? My friends ply her with compliments on her robe, the house. They feign interest in the show she's watching on the same television from when I was a kid, its gunked knobs only managing two channels.

"Is this the show with the retired baseball pitcher?"

"*Cheers.*" She pulls an envelope of cash from her pocket and hands it to me, face filled with hope.

I'd told her the money is for a school dance, invented of course. I knew she'd like the idea of me floating in crinoline layers grinding up on some law department dull-skin. I'd like to say I don't count the money while everyone waits, as if she'd short-change me.

These nameless friends wait on the lawn while I say goodbye.

"Tomorrow," my mother says. "Church?"

"Don't I come every Sunday?" I grimace toward the audience of sympathizers I imagine follow me.

"You do." She nods as if this is a reminder to herself that I'm not that bad.

"That's right I do."

As I leave, I catch her expression unfolding, energy surrendering, as if dealing with me requires a mask that slips farther the longer I stay. The punch of the recliner in the other room as she returns to her show is a dismissive sound signifying a crime that at nineteen I'm unable to articulate. Maybe it's indignation over the persona she dons to deal with me, her only daughter, that stops me on the lawn. I reenter the darkened family room to the sound of canned laughter.

"Thanks, I guess." For not saying a proper goodbye? For allowing me to leave angry.

Her baffled expression is lit by television. "What did I do?"

I let the screen door slam, join my friends, who are smoking cigarettes on the lawn, two easy hearts in the night.

We pile into my borrowed car and drive farther south in the city where the streets narrow. Dropping out had been surprisingly simple. I skipped a few classes, a few more, until college unhooked from me.

We arrive at the stadium bar where I've never once had a bad night and I'm thinking, I want to find a girl who looks correct in jeans, with a particular sag below her Donnas, our name for the bones above the pelvis.

A miracle happens and: I find her within minutes. Over the next few hours my friends recede into the crowd smiling against the wood-paneled walls. Each time the door opens I glimpse the strands of lights that garland the street, left over from the commemoration of Mary, known for falling into an hours-long ecstatic state, the girl says . . . Sounds great, I say, and she tells me it's not all it's cracked up to be. A high like that can only be followed by desolation. She's proud of the saint and her neighborhood, unable to hide her smile in the glances she offers me, at her beer. This loosens me, and I confess to lying about the money, my mother. I slap hands, buy drinks. I talk to everyone.

I wake on the floor of a dark room, phone and wallet gone, unsacred pulsing in my cheek. A switch plunges the room into a disagreeable light. A door and a shelf of books. A carpet of brown-and-red floral. What I slept against turns out to be a pool table.

Outside is an abbreviated hallway, the same sad sepia as the room. A bright bar shines at the end. I hear the din of talking. Two doors, marked LADIES and GENTS. A pay phone and framed newspaper clippings. A woman brushes past me, wearing a leopard sweater and a sequined barrette in the shape of a bow. I follow her to the bar, where the patrons welcome her with pleasant faces.

"Carla," the bartender says. "You look spiffy. You going out tonight?"

"Yep," she says. "Eddie and I are catching a movie. It's his last night in town. He's going out on the road again with the ice show."

"Uh-oh," says a man sitting at the bar.

She turns to him. "What's that supposed to mean?"

"Oh nothing. Well, you know. I got this image of chorus girls in skimpy costumes. Skating around. Lonely husband on the road far away from his connubial connubials. You're not worried?" They speak in bright tones and the man looks familiar; I may have borrowed a quarter from him the previous night for the jukebox.

"Not at all," the woman says. "I know my Eddie and I trust him completely." Anxious for her date, she walks to the front door, stops, calls over her shoulder. "He's the sweetest, most faithful loving husband in the whole world and I thank god every day he married me. If ever there was a one-woman man, it's Eddie LeBec."

A couple next to me converse in low tones. They ignore me when I ask for the time. I ask a suited man at the bar. Instead of answering, he yells to the woman, who pauses in the doorway. "Hey Carla, what movie you going to see?"

"*Fatal Attraction*." She leaves and climbs a flight of stairs that leads to the street, visible through a low window. The door closes. The first man nods to the second man. The lights in the bar dim. The chatting people around me lean against the brick wall and close their eyes. The bartender sits and seems to nap. Those seated around the bar place their heads on it as if powering down.

"My friends left and I just woke up in the back," I say to the first man. "Do you know what time it is?" Sliding his beer out of the way, he lays his cheek against the bar and closes his eyes.

In the darkness, a song plays above us on speakers I can't see. A man sings. It is the theme song from *Cheers*, my mother's favorite show. I recognize the actors though they look the same age as in the 1980s and '90s when the show was broadcast. I wasn't a fan but remember the bartender's name, Woody, and that the actor who played him went on to achieve box office success.

"When is it?" I ask an attractive yuppie woman, but she is sleeping against her partner's shoulder. "Where is this? I have to take my mother to church." I realize I'm dreaming. I will wake up, probably on the floor of the previous night's bar, get home, figure out the money later.

"Wake up," I instruct myself.

The song ends. The lights return.

Sam Malone, former famous baseball pitcher who ruined his career with drink, stands behind the bar with Woody. They study Sam's wristwatch. A brunette woman enters and announces that she has just returned from a seminar in which she has learned how to speak effectively on her own behalf. When she is finished asserting herself, they count down from five. On one, the bar explodes into cheering. No one has been listening to the woman. They've been waiting for a specific moment to arrive. The people around me pump their fists and cheer.

"What's going on?" I say, the same time the woman says, "What's going on?" We are both ignored.

Wake up, I order myself.

Sam explains that today is the second anniversary of their only recorded win against a rival bar, Gary's Old Town Tavern.

Gary's staff had humiliated them in a variety of sports until two years before, when the Cheers bar bested them in bowling. Carla, the waitress who not five minutes before left to see *Fatal Attraction*, emerges from the back holding a trophy that she parades around the bar.

I take a seat while Sam calls Gary to remind him of the auspicious anniversary. "This moment of victory is frozen in time." Hanging up, he realizes that the trophy is missing. Sam and Woody leave for Gary's to retrieve the stolen trophy and moments later reenter carrying the trophy, broken in half. Cheers vows revenge. A series of pranks ensues. The gang becomes suspicious of everyone coming into the bar.

Wake up, I beg.

The scene ends. The lights dim and the people power down. Interlude music plays.

My vision narrows and my breath comes out serrated. I fill a glass with water and press myself into a booth in the corner. I've had panic attacks but never a fully wrought sensory delusion. Yet this anxiety theater has no seam I can find. The walls reach the ceiling, the floors are finished, even the details, the pretzels in the bowl. The framed sports articles from Boston newspapers. My riddled brain has unspooled a perfect replica.

Dr. Frasier Crane and his wife, Lilith, enter arguing. Dr. Crane warns the crew against retaliation.

The pranks continue. Extras shift and move around the set, whispering nothing. I am able to touch and move things, but no one sees or hears me. Panicking, I lose track of the storyline and am only barely aware of Gary entering, feigning a truce with the brunette, then filling her office with sheep. Carla appears from the back room, dressed in black and holding a toolbox.

At the end of the episode, the cast pumps and whistles around the bar cheering "We're number one."

"Pretty weenie," says Al, a callback to an earlier joke. Everyone looks knowingly at him and at one another.

The lights dim. The ensemble closes their eyes. The theme song plays again, a lone, plaintive oboe replacing the singer. When it finishes, the lights go out. Bright sax erupts from the speakers. The lights return, and Carla emerges from the back room, wearing the leopard sweater and sequin bow.

Woody says, "Carla, you look spiffy. You going out tonight?"

The episode begins again.


When Dr. Crane and Lilith enter arguing, I run through the front door but at the top of the stairs am halted by a brick wall. I try escaping through the back window, hurl a pilsner, climb the steps to Melville's, the seafood restaurant whose entrance is inside the bar. I see a reservations desk but, reaching the last step, find myself on a wooden platform, a staircase on the other side leading back down to the set.

"Pretty weenie." The episode ends. Lights down. Lights up. The episode begins.


As I've done with every hard thing in my life—father, friendships—I become a student, analyzing my situation with the acute care of self-pity. I memorize and inspect every set piece for exit, the phony Tiffany lamps like jeweled mushrooms, ashtrays, bouquets of red straws arranged along the bar, two ferns, antlers. I'm in a later episode, after the popular character of Coach has died and been replaced by Woody, the mild-mannered Indiana boy, and after the fussy blond woman is replaced by the brunette who is fussy in a different way.

THIS IS A SQUARE HOUSE, a sign reads. PLEASE REPORT ANY UNFAIRNESS TO THE PROPRIETOR.

An hour of implied time passes when Sam and Carla go to Gary's to dole out dribble glasses then return to the bar. Between Carla leaving on her mission and Gary visiting the bar to admit defeat, an entire evening, morning, and afternoon "pass." *Who is running lights and sound? Who is replenishing the bowls of olives and pretzels?* I develop and nourish theories on my captors. I rule out the girl who looked good in jeans, my friends, even my mother, as time passes in half-hour increments. The actors show no signs of being complicit. Their makeup remains fresh. Their hair poised in the gravity-defying styles of the 1980s.

The loop is predictable and after several hours fades into background static. Certain phrases refuse to dematerialize, buoys in a monotonous sea. THIS MOMENT OF VICTORY IS FROZEN IN TIME, Sam tells Gary during the anniversary phone call. IT'S REALLY RATHER MACHIAVELLIAN, Dr. Crane says about the final prank. When Carla asks why Norm and Cliff are seated at the bar like a bunch of wimps, Norm says, THAT'S WHAT WIMPS DO. Each replay is launched by CARLA, YOU LOOK SPIFFY and finishes with PRETTY WEENIE. These phrases continue as I sleep under the pool table, marking literal and implied time in my dreams, only to awake in agony to find myself again in rerun.

A stranger from Framingham enters the bar. He wears a gentleman's suit, thinning hair swept to the side in worry. He has stopped in for a beer because, he explains, his wife is getting surgery at a nearby hospital. The gang circles him, assuming he's been sent by Gary to Vaseline the benches or unscrew the salt shakers. "Sick wife, yeah right," they keen, they arrow. The stranger from Framingham does not understand why he is being viewed with suspicion. With the hope of finding relief from the devastation of loss, he has accidentally wandered into a bar whose denizens are engaged in a prank war with a rival bar. He speaks with the exhaustion of grief. He leaves the bar as the regulars snarl.

During this time, the sheep are the closest thing to friends I have, though they are only present for ten minutes at a time. I pet and confide in them. I miss Philadelphia, I tell them. They are on a shorter loop. One nuzzles another, prompting a third to take a step back. Every few moments the same nuzzle, the same retraction. I don't fault them for their predictability. They are more reliable than my human friends. The fussy brunette enters and, seeing them, throws the papers she'd been holding into the air. The sheep disappear when the door slams. One moment I am surrounded by the softly lowing, dung-smelling bodies of animals, the next I am alone.

I pick up the bar phone. No dial tone.

The episode contains twelve entrances and eleven exits through the front door. During each one, I attempt escape only to encounter the same brick walls. I vary timing, speed, approach. Over and over, the set returns me to itself. I feel every inch of the brick walls for hinges to reveal hidden rooms, but the moorings hold.

"I'm lonely," I tell the sheep, but they are caught in their own loop and cannot help.

I hurl bowls of olives against the wall. I spend a full minute screaming during the phone call scene. No matter how I disturb the set, it subsumes my efforts and replaces itself. Beers return within seconds. No matter how I muscle the actors, they return to their intended path.

IT'S REALLY RATHER MACHIAVELLIAN.

THAT'S WHAT WIMPS DO.

I keep track of the replays by carving hash marks on a back wall with a bar knife. I reach 1,500 episodes, twenty-seven minutes each. Almost a month of human time spent eating bar olives and pretzels, the replenishment of which I no longer wonder about. Instead, I agonize over my real life, proceeding unmanned. Un-me-ed. Is it progressing in real or sitcom time, or in some unknown, third way? In leaps, in gasps. If I ever return, will decades or weeks have passed?

The stranger from Framingham is the only character who is motivated by an unselfish goal. Every episode I wait for him, mouth his lines, and am sad when he leaves unexpectedly, inevitably. I think of his wife in the ICU, his attempt to curb anxiety, thwarted by the suspicion sparked by childish pranks. "Do you have children?" I ask him. "Do you enjoy watching movies?" He never answers. In the manner of unrequited relationships, I project my desire onto the blank screen of him. Oh, stranger from Framingham. Your hours at the hospital are torment. You are a hardworking man who has had one extramarital partner. You worry that this flagging of morals has cancered your wife.

"I'm trapped in a rerun," I tell him. "Please tell your wife."

———

Three-quarters of the way through every replay, responding to an internal mechanism the way daylilies activate in sun, Carla appears in the back room in her soldier outfit, then waits by the pay phone for her cue. She will exit through the front room and travel the implied three blocks to Gary's, where she will tap into his cable box so he is unable to broadcast the night's big fight. Instead, his bar patrons will see a taped video of Cliff and Norm, pretending to host an evening of poetry. I've given up hissing at her. I can touch but not move her.

I am depressed, insecure, and petulant. My theories break and bend. I spend most of my time under the pool table, listening to the beats, marking time by Carla's entrances and exits. Are people at home watching this episode in some predawn rerun seeing me weep next to the overly rouged group of yuppies whispering nothing? If only I'd been a better daughter. I could sway on the dance floor with someone upstanding and not hang out in a bar with losers.

One half hour, Dr. Crane "sees" me.

The gang retreats but he keeps his gaze trained on me. "Who are you?"

I tell him my name and my situation and ask if he can help me escape. "I want to get home to my mother."

"Many times, we speak a different language from our parents. We address our mothers from a stubborn set of assumptions and never really try to translate into their understanding.

This is akin to executing perfect tennis strokes on different courts. Gives a whole new meaning to mother tongue." He chuckles softly.

"I'll try any stroke you want if I can get out of here."

"You are trapped in your circumstances. We must be wary of what we find ourselves repeating. What is it you're attempting to obfuscate? Finish this sentence: Repeating behavior makes me feel . . ."

"Can you get a message to someone when you go back to your apartment?"

"A grace note is harmonically inessential, yet sometimes it's the only way to hear that a pattern has been broken."

"Please help," I say.

"A potentially unending cycle of juvenile retaliation could only lead to a kind of mob mentality which will ultimately result in a regrettable act." He's speaking to the group, who have remained frozen while we speak. Lights up.

The episode continues.


The episode needs nothing from me, so it becomes as innocuous as a public park I spend my days in. One afternoon during the final scene, as the gang cheers WE'RE NUMBER ONE, I pick up the bar phone.

A woman's voice says, "Melville's? Would you like to make a reservation?"

"Yes," I say. "God, yes."

"For what time?"

"Six?"

The line goes dead. I scream hello.

During the next episode I pace the bar. When the gang celebrates their victory, I pick up the phone. Again, the woman asks if I'd like a reservation. I try for one at noon. The line dies, leaving me devastated, invigorated.

I spend the next few episodes trying different reservation times. Each one elicits a hang up. I puzzle out my options in the pool room. When would I realistically be able to eat dinner at Melville's in the real time of the show?

Carla enters and, like she has thousands of times, checks the toolbox, left to right, clamps the lid, moves into the hallway to wait by the pay phone for her cue, holding the videocassette of Norm and Cliff's phony evening of poetry.

Evening of poetry! There is only one implied evening in the real time of the show when the patrons of Gary's Old Town Tavern expect to watch the fight but are duped.

In the bar, the cast is powered down before the last scene. I wait at the edge, a girl poised to jump into double Dutch. Finally, inevitably, again, the conflict resolves and the gang reaches their sad-sack conclusion.

They cheer, "We're number one!"

I pick up the phone.

"Melville's?" the woman says.

"I'd like to make a reservation."

"For what time?"

"Last night at 7:00 p.m."

"Very good, ma'am. We'll see you then."

I hang up, stunned by success. I parade around the bar with the gang, high-stepping and wagging my hips, until the oboe signals the end of a full arc of human experience, and we return to our places of rest.

Since I am convinced this is my last replay, every joke seems well-timed and hilarious. I guffaw at the punch lines. When the stranger from Framingham enters, he is a memory of a former self who once loved him. Goodbye to that self. Goodbye, Woody. Goodbye, pretty weenie. These people never knew me but by sheer time accrued, they are my colleagues.

Carla waits in the hallway for her third-act cue. I whisper, "Goodbye, Carla. I hope Eddie returns from his business trip soon."

Her eyes remain on the bar. Her smell, Halloween candy and mahogany. Her heart thrums in a vein that lines her throat. This is as satisfactory a goodbye as any other. Hearing Sam's whistle, she answers into the bar. I follow. "Toolbox, check. Tape, check." The brunette's familiar protests of illegality. Carla exits. The remaining cast powers down and I climb the interior steps to Melville's. The reservation desk shines at the top. The wink of glass on tables. Fear slows me. Will I again find only a platform and a staircase forcing me back to set? But as I advance the desk grows sharper, the way it would in a set that was unending—the real world, I mean.

"Welcome to Melville's," the woman says. "Do you have a reservation?"

My legs fail, I clutch the podium for support. Yes, I cry. The door to the street is mere yards away. I run, flinching, anticipating a brick wall or canopy of hands dragging me back. I wrench it open, leap through, and find myself on a city street in a perfect, ordinary afternoon. Around me, nothing but Boston. Cars pass. Two identical men in contemporary clothing jog by, startling me. A child dashes his leg against a pole. Satin air and the honking of horns and the kid, once the shock wears off, crying. Trees in a park a few blocks away. Random, spontaneous life! A cab squeals to a halt because I have stepped in front of it. The driver smiles into the rearview mirror when I slide into the back seat.

"Can you see me?" I say.

Her brow furrows. "I can see you just fine."

The relief at hearing unscripted words. I want to talk and talk. "When is it?" I ask and she tells me it's June.

"June!" I say. "Thank god." I sink farther into the seat, watching the city stream by. Unchoreographed people jogging. My mother will make me grilled cheese with avocado and sprouts. I will tell her what happened and everything will return to normal.

"Must have been some day," the cabdriver says. "Where to?"

There's a narrow cobblestone street, I tell her. In the city of Philadelphia. Can she take me there? "That's where my mother lives."

But as we drive, worry grows. Will I find her, still sixty-five, or will she have aged and died, wondering why I abandoned her? If she is alive, can I be certain that where I am finding her is the genuine article, or will I be in some other Philadelphia that has spun off the world that's kept me captive? Is my mother asleep on the couch dreaming me while in real life I am ambling up to her house with my detrimental friends? Will this cab exit the turnpike to find a pile of cardboard boxes and a sign reading CITY HERE with an arrow, a brick wall, the edge of some television writer's line of thinking?

Philadelphia, incredibly, exists. When we see its gray hulking mass spread along the horizon my eyes fill with tears. We wind through its cobblestone streets, hushed in twilight. Nearing my mother's house, I am filled with sudden, leaden woe. I can't fathom why I directed the driver to this place. "On second thought," I say, "there's a bar a few blocks away. I'll have a drink then make my visit."

As if to pacify her, I add, "I promise."

Why can't I look straight at it? Mother: A trembling, dark spot. Swatting at flies with a rolled *TV Guide*. She'll find me filthy and manic. She who has never entered a bar, let alone longed for one. Yet I don't want redemption. I want a cool place where people speak with the gentle tone of colleagues. We don't know much about each other but are kinder than family; offering a quarter for the jukebox, a light remark, a joke that doesn't cut too deep, a glass of whiskey to settle my relentless, shattered nerves.

# The Night Gardener

The first balloon arrives at midnight when Claudia is gardening. It is late summer in Pennsylvania, and the bats are already gone. The short-eared owls and the sandpiper, too. The last known family of great egrets has recently produced a clutch of eggs. They live in a park near Claudia, on the edge of the city. She is nagging the rhododendron roots, thinking about their wide white wings when she senses a figure behind her. A green balloon hovers, lilting on its string, as if summoning the courage to speak. Claudia opens a folded ecru paper stapled to its neck and reads the patient, handwritten scrawl: HELLO.

"Hello," Claudia says.

How long had it been there, levitating over a pile of discarded lily ends? Where had it come from? The yards to her left and right are person-less; the woods that border the yard empty. A deer that had checked on her earlier is gone. Hands covered in earth, Claudia uses her forearm to manage a brow itch. Even the clouds seemed paused, to wonder.

Only a week remains before the Horticultural Society will judge her in the City Gardens Contest. Claudia had been hoping to finish before the rain.

Collecting discarded lily ends signals the end of her gardening session and though she loves it—the sealing in of the night's practice—she is sorry for the work to be over. She considers herself an assistant to unburdening, trimming stems of wasted energy. The bodies of the dead lilies are cool against her palm as she hangs her tools in the shed. The balloon flinches, flicked invisibly on all sides; the first raindrops. Claudia pulls the balloon inside the house. Before bed, she reads a few pages of her nocturnal farming digest. In one of the photos, a line of combines harvest grain in a staggered formation at night, hulking their sieves through a field under powerful headlights. It is an aerial view, the machines fall down the image diagonally. Their conical beams light the wild, moving wheat in front; the furrowed field left in darkness behind. They look like spaceships, Claudia thinks.

In the morning, Claudia's thighs are sore. She likes when the previous night's work visits upon her body. In the garden that afternoon, a blue balloon twists in the branches of her willow tree. Claudia braces the ladder against the trunk and climbs. She unwinds its measure from the hanging vines. A folded card identical to the first is stapled to its string.

YOU SEEM LONELY.

The moon and yard provide no answer. Internet searches (spam balloons, balloon messages while gardening) prove fruitless.

That evening, Claudia peers at Raj through the peephole. He wears dark jeans and holds a sleeve of peonies and two silver metallic balloons: HAPPY 4TH BIRTHDAY. Behind him a student drifts by in a Cutlass Ciera. A nearby driving school owns a fleet of them, roofs outfitted with enormous STUDENT DRIVER signs.

"I thought it was funny," Raj says.

Claudia met Raj at her data entry job. The promise she felt

when they began dating has transformed into a two-sided gem; in some lights flashing boredom and in others disgust.

"Is this your house?" he says, following her inside.

Claudia does not understand the question. He gestures to the green and blue balloons in the corner kowtowing from air loss. "Looks like someone got here before me."

Claudia makes a simple dinner of greens and avocado and shows him the cards that landed with the balloons. Raj does not suspect anything mysterious. He explains that the local grade school holds field days when students write messages on balloons they release simultaneously. He participated when he attended. There had probably been a balloon release a few days before, he reasons.

Claudia attended a school that did not have field day. "That sounds horrible for the environment."

He laughs and says most balloons never make it out of the parking lot. One year his was popped by a power line. She appreciates that he does not use the occasion of remembrance to brag. Yet his story feels like a dismissal of her balloons, and she doesn't like the metallic ones he brought that shine against the ceiling like cleavers.

"Thank you for the peonies," she says. It is meant as a closing remark that will propel him to leave.

"Irises," he says.

She takes a picture of the flowers and texts it to her sister: WHAT KIND OF FLOWERS ARE THESE? "No one knows more about flowers than my sister."

He seems pleased they will have a future reason to talk, but Claudia knows she will not update him. He leaves. Relieved, she slits the Mylar balloons with scissors, squeezes them airless against the counter, and junks them. Loyalty. She imagines the green and blue balloons nodding in approval.

After midnight, she is winding a cucumber vine through a trellis when she feels a blow against the top of her head. She's been buzzed by a—it cannot be. A bat makes wild arcs through the garden. Claudia thought all of the bats were gone but this one is as real as she, slicing the air with its might, making inquiries of each bank of branches. Its searching takes it to the treetops; a small, black, beating muscle pounding back reality above her. Even as it pauses at the farthest edge of every arc to reposition for the return, allowing her to take in its unmistakable grips and wingspan, she cannot believe in it.

Claudia began to garden at night because of the heat index but had developed an instant love for its weatherlessness, its sense of hovering and secrecy. She liked that the night yard contained only a handful of sounds and that they were natural sounds: the yeps of the toads and the katydids' measured counting, though she missed birdsong. The day's colors could be garish and over-whelming but at night she dealt in placid greens and navies, the occasional sheen of her trowel under the moon, but mostly gentle dark. In the dark her hands were untroubling ideas working the soil where unearthed worms burrowed into deeper earth. She liked the air's cold, firm hand, and that she almost always entered the house shaking with exhaustion, skin coated in a mist she hadn't felt collecting. One gardening session ended when, star-tled as if from reverie, Claudia found herself surrounded by the rattles and whoops of morning birds. The world seemed kinder at night, and she was more susceptible to that kindness. Like the moon lilies that wait until the sun has set to speak.

This is the first year Claudia has entered the City Gardens Contest. First prize is a professional rain gauge. The runner-up receives a five-dollar gift certificate to a garden supply store.

A few members fussed because Claudia lives on the outer edge of the city in a freestanding house. I pay city taxes, she typed in a letter, I have a city zip code. It worked. In a few days, senior members will judge the area of land she has ordered and trimmed based on her taste and talent.

In the yard the next morning, Claudia jumps for an arriving yellow balloon.

Behind it, timed like a passenger jet, an orange.

The yellow balloon's card reads:

DO YOU LIKE YOUR LIFE?

The orange:

WE ARE VERY SCARED.

The messages are not what a grade schooler would write, but Claudia dials the elementary school and leaves a message. She excavates her art supplies from her basement, cuts a small square of paper, and writes:

MY NAME IS CLAUDIA ROSE. I AM A BROWN DATA ENTRY CLERK AND I DO NOT LIKE MY LIFE. WHY ARE YOU SCARED?

Claudia removes the card that reads DO YOU LIKE YOUR LIFE?, replaces it with her reply, and releases the balloon. It sends itself out of the yard on its original path, lit dimly by the waning moon.

She pulls the lawn mower from the shed but after several tries must accept it is broken. She can't afford a new one. She remembers reading about a nocturnal farming collective that trimmed what was left of their grass with scissors. A photograph: Young people holding slim, delicate shears, on their hands and knees, constellated over a lawn.

The next evening, a red balloon arrives:

WE ARE SORRY YOU DO NOT LIKE YOUR LIFE.

A few minutes later, a pink:

WE ARE UNDER ATTACK.

Lighthearted with romance, Claudia sends:

I AM NOT RARE. MOST AMERICANS DON'T LIKE THEIR LIVES NOW. MANY OF US ARE SCARED TOO.

Wanting to express interest in the person or people sending the cards, she adds:

WHO ARE YOU? WHO IS ATTACKING YOU?

She watches the balloon sail out of the yard, flirt through the willow branches and the gap between the electric poles, over the maple copse furred in heat.

Later, she watches the news and boils water for spaghetti. The American bittern is gone. The black-crowned night heron and the long-eared owl. The great egret eggs should hatch within the week. The mother and father take turns incubating. Volunteers camp beneath the tree, shooing climate tourists. The president stoops to receive a golden necklace on the other side of the world. Claudia wonders if her balloon friends live near the faraway country, where gay people and dissidents are beheaded. She never should have watched that infamous video. What does it say about her, that it was at once more and less brutal than she anticipated?

Claudia's job requires her to spend several hours seated at a desk in a climate-controlled office. She inputs sheets of names and addresses into a massive spreadsheet. The names belong to older people who sold their life insurance policies to Claudia's company in exchange for a lump sum. Claudia only feels awake at night, kneeling under a variation of the moon.

The next evening, before leaving for a data entry clerk happy hour, Claudia crawls across her yard, snipping the grass with her sister's vintage scissors. A black balloon arrives:

WE DO NOT HAVE MUCH TIME. IN A FEW DAYS WE WILL BE GONE OH WELL.

A purple balloon:

THE BIRTHMARK ON YOUR NECK IS LOVELY.

Claudia sends back:

HOW CAN I HELP?

The balloon vaults the maple copse before making a purposeful retraction, as if asking itself a question, then answers through the opening made from two electric poles, skirts the willow, and investigates a farther breeze.

She waits for a response until she must get dressed.

The bar is in the basement of a local housing complex. Her manager has ordered chicken fingers, chicken wings, and chicken nuggets for the team. Plates of them are spread around the cocktail tables. Claudia nurses a whiskey and listens to gossip regarding a new associate. She longs to be home, scanning her backyard for balloons. Please let there be a balloon when I get home. She retreats into the bathroom to press a fingertip against her birthmark, waiting as if for a lover's text.

"Such a nice spread," one of her coworkers says, meaning the fingers, wings, and nuggets.

"Unless you're a chicken," Claudia says. "At which point it'd be like a house of horror."

"You've been absent-minded all week," another clerk says. "Messing up your twos and fours."

"Love," guesses another clerk. She winks at Raj across the room, who grins, winks back.

Claudia announces she will leave. Explains about the garden, the lawn, the contest.

"What does a professional rain gauge do?" the coworker says.

"It measures rain."

The coworker glances toward the window. "Not much to measure these days."

Outside the bar Claudia takes a picture of a large tree with green stalks topped by wild yellow lilies. A tiger lily variant? She's never seen one so large. She texts the picture to her sister: WHAT FLOWER IS THIS?

On her street, Claudia gets stuck behind a student driver creeping down the road. Feeling selfish and warranted, she leans on her horn with the rigor of shame. But at home there are no balloons. She sleeps crosswise on the bed, still in her go-out clothes.

———

Raj wakes her and tells her to dress quickly, there is something she must see. They are in the empty parking lot of a featureless concrete building. At a side door, Raj backhands a curtain to reveal a room retrofitted to hold an enormous churning machine. Pumping and whistling, it produces her ecru cards, dozens a minute. They churn and spit and replicate, piles stacked to the ceiling. Raj hands her a few to read. YOU SEEM LONELY. HELLO. WE ARE VERY SCARED. YOUR BIRTHMARK. YOUR THROAT. O DEAREST CLAUDIA.

You're one of many, Raj says. You are not rare.

Claudia feels betrayed, furious. The noise of the machine grows louder. The stacks grow. Claudia, Raj, and the room are suddenly underwater. Claudia swims to catch a student driver passing at the edge of the lot.

"Come back." Raj swims after her. "You must stop telling yourself stories."

Being able to admonish her through water feels like a practical ability only he would have, which infuriates her more. Claudia paddles furiously but the car remains the same distance away.


The next evening, a white balloon arrives:

YOU CANNOT HELP US IT WILL SOON BE OVER THANK YOU.

A lavender:

EMBRACE EMERGING EXPERIENCE.

Claudia resents the flimsy spirituality, something she could crack out of a fortune cookie. Lack of sleep makes her skittery and mean.

I HATE THE PEOPLE WHO ARE SCARING YOU.

She sends it and turns to her garden things, intending to busy herself. She cannot spend another day distracted by worry. A few minutes later, a new balloon floats behind her. Her scream is so loud it makes her laugh.

WE DO NOT WANT YOU TO HATE THOSE WHO HATE US.

Claudia gazes at the sky. She writes: WHAT CAN I DO?

She neatens the yard, locks the house, and drives to the twenty-four-hour supermarket. On a vine blooming over the mangled shopping cart gate, burgundy trumpets lift toward the moon. She texts a photo to her sister: WHAT FLOWER IS THIS?

She purchases a dozen balloons and drives home where she attaches cards and brings them to the backyard.

She releases the first:

TELL ME WHAT TO DO.

The second:

TELL ME WHAT TO DO.

The third, fourth, and fifth, etc. . . .

The activity clears her anxiety, enabling her to pull weeds. She stands in the middle of the garden at dusk, holding a hose.

No balloons arrive.

Days pass.

Claudia feels too big for her body. She doesn't know where to put herself. She tries the bathroom, the kitchen, the yard. Her life before the balloons feels like it belonged to someone else. Let nature take the garden, she thinks. It is obscene, anyway, to force plants to do one's bidding, to pretend that ordering a plot of flowers will stave off whatever's coming.

Raj visits, holding another metallic balloon. On it he has stapled a card that reads: I'M IN LOVE WITH CLAUDIA. Her lack of interest has clarified his desire.

"At least let me see the garden," he says, gleaning her disappointment.

He follows her to the yard where the grass is half trimmed, half wild. "Mower's broke," she says.

He gazes at the portulaca, the willow, the lilies. His voice is respectful, careful. "How did you learn to garden like this?"

"My sister," she says.

"She must be so proud."

Claudia is too tired to protect his experience. "She's dead."

"But you," he says, "texted her the other night?"

"It wouldn't be fair if everything had to end when someone dies."

He seems to expect a longer explanation, but she can't help if it's not simple for him, and she cannot forgive him for the dream. A weed. After he leaves, she murders the Mylar balloon and throws it and the card into the trash.

The evening news reports the great egret eggs failed to hatch. Too much time has elapsed, it is hopeless. The father has vanished. The mother refuses to surrender her station. The newscast shows footage of her, head tucked into a wide pale wing, a bright smear on a mirror. Claudia looks onto the front street hoping a leaping cat will appear or a sudden downpour or even a student driver pausing underneath the streetlight to gather strength. But there is only a trash can wearing a flattened box like a hat. Not even a moon.


Claudia drives to the local elementary school. The receptionist reads the cards and agrees it's strange. She looks up the last field day and finds there hasn't been one for twenty years, since

Raj was a student. She shows Claudia a photograph from the final one and tsks over the image of smiling children holding balloons on a vast lawn. "Grass and balloons. Terrible for the environment."

Claudia feels vindicated. "That's what I said."

A tree hangs over the parking lot, heavy with an embarrassment of flowers. Falling over one another, enough for every branch plus extra. The richness of its lemony fragrance catches in Claudia's throat as she holds up her phone.

Claudia drives home, mind buzzing with theories. Could the balloons be from that last field day, delayed? Or replicated by some lonely person with a helium tank? It occurs to her to be scared but the balloons seem friendly, altruistic; receiving them felt like being regarded with neutrality. Someone curious who does not wish to intrude. The way the deer check her when she gardens. Intending nothing more threatening than *You, there*. For a moment, she allows herself to imagine her sister is sending them. From heaven or some other, more believable place.

A Cutlass Ciera coasts by, piloted by a driver filled with fear.

The messages use "we" but Claudia does not rule out the source being one person. She knows that we-ness can be a singular experience. Further, that one person can contain many.

Claudia enters the house feeling deflated. She pours a tumbler of water and stands at the counter, drinking, gazing through the window to the yard. The Horticultural Society people will arrive in the morning and the grass is still overgrown. This, plus her address-related shaky standing plus the tenuous strand that separates newbies from veterans could mean disqualification. After a hasty dinner, Claudia spends hours crouched in the yard, clipping the grass manually. The grass soaks through her jeans as she moves around the maple, the rhododendron, Siberian iris, and portulaca. The woods are dark. Fireflies point things out on the lawn. Ordinarily, their gentle lamps would fill Claudia with ease, however fireflies are an insult when all she wants are balloons.

An hour has passed when a huff of sound retracts Claudia's attention into sharp focus. Dark bodies surround her in the dark. She remains motionless and catches glimpses of them in parts: Shining eyes, a muscled torso, the flick of a tail. Their hesitant breath. She senses the others waiting behind farther trees. The deer move past her into the forest. In the center of their party, a dew-slick fawn tests new legs. The others shield and teach with their unhurried movement. Claudia doesn't move until the final one, a doe that faces her until her family is through, turns and with a showy leap rejoins them.

This is no receipt of new information. Yet the clarity of this encounter, the clap of moisture against her palms, prompts an inarguable feeling of dread.

The great egret father is hit by a motorist traveling to the mountain festival. The son of the driver catches the entire encounter on film. The father egret swoops too low over the highway. The collision tears one of its wings. Beating the remaining wing, it attempts to ascend and is hit by a second car.

Claudia turns the news off. Her face is hot with anger. What is the worst part? That she had seen the bird in pieces? Or that even after being hit he was still trying to fly?

Three pale, blazered women holding thick pads of paper glare into the sun. They decline glasses of water and the colorful plates of food Claudia had laid out as they file into the yard. None of them live in the city, she discovers through small talk, but descend from the suburbs to judge the city gardens that usually happen in window boxes or rooftops or in communal plots.

They scribble notes as they move around her work. Claudia stifles the urge to explain every plant. They commiserate under the maple as she un- then rewinds the hose.

"Good," one of them says. "Except for the rhododendron situation."

"Situation?" Claudia says.

They glance at one another before one of them says, "Dead, of course."

"What is your definition of dead?" Claudia says.

"Unable to produce new growth—"

"Get on your hands and knees and look at the work I did."

They look at the ground.

"This is bullshit," Claudia says before realizing she will say it. "You come in here and judge my garden?"

The judges consult each other. "That's our job."

"For a lousy rain gauge?" Claudia makes a shooing gesture. She no-thank-yous the judges out of the garden.

One of the women pauses at the fence. "It's a very good rain gauge. Professional grade."

"There's nothing to gauge!" Claudia says.

The judges retreat to a boxy car parked in front of the house as a student driver glides by, pumping the brake. One of the judges, waiting for her colleague to unlock her door, does not see him and is clipped. Two collisions: the bird and the judge. For a moment,

Claudia conflates them. There is an unsettling thumping sound, and no screaming.

Late that evening, Claudia returns from the hospital. The judge had been only bruised, but it had been an upsetting experience for her, her fellow judges, and the student, who followed them to the hospital at a glacial pace, signaling when it wasn't necessary and taking too long to park. He is likely ruined for driving. Claudia's membership to the Horticultural Society has been revoked, a decision she agrees is best for everyone.

In the kitchen, Claudia pours a tumbler of water she immediately drops. It shatters against the floor. The garden is filled with balloons. Hundreds of colors and strings. An undulating body consisting of separate parts, flashing in moonlight.

Claudia runs outside and gathers as many as she can. Relieved to tearfulness, she unfolds the first note with shaking fingers. The next and the next. Each bears the same message, hitting harder with each repetition. She clambers to reach the ones stuck in the maple, the power lines. Maybe one will say they survived. Maybe one will contain what she needs, a location, a reason, a point. But she finds only the same violent fold, again and again, hundreds, an onslaught, bearing the same painful, impossible thought: CLAUDIA, FILL YOUR HEART WITH LOVE.

# Kathleen in Light Colors

○

Before I knew you, I had a lover I could not feel.

I mean this literally—between Kathleen and me existed an unseen body that moved when we did. Body is the wrong word. The entity was something and nothing, a/an _____. We discovered it the first time we made love, a muted affair. Touching her felt like plunging my hands into water. She said touching me felt like wearing mittens.

We tried different times and locations, hoping to outsmart the _____. Menstruation, noon. Fire escape, vestibule, pool. Still, the _____ divided us, an invisible obfuscating blanket. A third party.

We talked about the _____ as if it were a coworker with baffling motives. Was it my late father continuing what he started in life—punishing my strong will? Kathleen's criminal brother, up to tricks? A supernatural ex wishing to exclude us from love's country? She remained friendly with all of hers, and mine were too lazy to bother.

I'd read that armpit glands excrete slicks that smell like sourdough during perimenopause—we were both the right age. Or was it extreme dehydration? Besides draining bottles of Malbec every night, we were healthy.

The _____ never slacked or slept. Assigning it human attributes most likely misled our efforts. Neither of us imagined it could have supernatural origin.

Kathleen was determined to solve this romantic mystery but I tired of the talking, content to leave space for the unknown. I considered the _____ an alchemy that occurred when we two were together, the way on some neck vetiver smells like rancid apple. Whatever hovers outside our understanding and whatever hovers outside that? Cool.

Hoping to catch the _____ unaware, Kathleen would hurl herself at me in bed or in public. She touched me constantly but never reached me. I was overly kneaded, undersexed.

Other than the _____, life proceeded normally. Near misses with sunsets, subway disagreements. Dinners, some good. Every so often, her brother called to demand an audience to his escapades and she'd meet him on some faraway train platform. Every so often, J.Crew emailed to inform me they'd reinvented the polo shirt. Kathleen and I spent hours reading—her historical biography, me horror erotica. Whatever it was manifested as distance we regarded each other through or over. She worked as a customer service representative and every night would come to my house and deliver a kiss through glass. We had discounted tickets to one another, obstructed view. We couldn't have known what would have been better without the _____, what it allowed us to see only half of. From what thorny partnership issues did working on the puzzle of it distract us?

At last, she surrendered, and it became relationship architecture, like her insistence we eat outside and my tendency to say "You can never truly know." This phrase enabled me to forgive all manner of ills, usually those committed upon me: A man who lied about his height, friends who sided with the bully, a mother whose love got caught in her throat. I used this phrase because

I wanted to continue liking the person, which I guess means I wanted to continue liking the world.

One night, a couple we knew who lived on opposite coasts came for dinner. They said distance like darkness invents monsters. A malevolent goblin where there is only a coat thrown over a chair. They said we must compensate for what circumstance removed by articulating everything, mundane to profound. Words would nullify the distance.

Later, while drying dishes, Kathleen asked if I'd ever wondered what the _____ would look like if it decided to reveal itself.

She was certain: intarsia. Mostly red, all shades brick to jelly bean to the maroon burst I felt when she piled the laundry on top of the full basket instead of readying the bags for drop-off. I realized I too was certain: White with dappled black, like the face of a character in an old film peering through a boardinghouse's slatted shade. The forest floor in monochrome. She didn't like old movies. I didn't know what intarsia was. This was perhaps an indicator of deeper incompatibilities.

If it decided to reveal itself. Here we were imposing human logic again. What ego! We assumed invisibility was a defensive action and in other circumstances it was corporal, visible. We never considered it was, simply, clear.

Not everyone feels the same about darkness. Darkness for me means safe. My father couldn't come for me if I hid in the bathroom cupboard. The metaphor that would have worked for me was, this entity sheds so much light you cannot do the adult equivalent of hide, which is posture.

I was love's trouper, so I talked.

I said, "I'm sliding my hand up your hot thigh, between your legs where you're so, so wet."

She said, "I'm feeling the results of your yoga practice! You've really been putting in effort!"

That's when I discovered she was bad with words.

Undaunted, I articulated wider, deeper.

"I feel a trapdoor in the skin underneath my fingertips. If I press down, I'll access where you carry pain."

She said, "That's just a muscle spasm."

We continued our efforts to apprehend each other through all but one of the senses. I described every possible sensation. She stated what was literally happening. No matter how we tried to gain linguistic purchase, we were still wearing oven mitts.

Neither of us made the other come the entire year. You know me; I don't fake. Mutual masturbation was all we had.


Finally, we visited the neighborhood occult shop to inquire about our condition. They employed a cunning woman who specialized in romantic woes. This was New York, so she was booked. During the week we had to wait, I felt sheepish around the _____, knowing we were about to eradicate it. If my desires had cooled, Kathleen's had tripled. She said after it left she was going to dig her hands into me for hours. She chomped the heads off carrots, took howling-hot baths.

I was frightened.

Our meeting with the cunning woman the following week was professional, a mole-removal procedure, with more candles.

Kathleen detailed our situation with holy, quaking eyes. "A river divides us," she said. "A thick pane of glass."

The cunning woman dismissed our dramatics with a shrug. "Some people have shadows." Inside a chalk circle, she addressed us and the _____. She warned that its departure would be uneventful, like mist clearing. But there was a rent in the air, a sudden upheaval in energy, and a sorrowful sound. Goodbye?

Hearing the _____'s pain, as you no doubt already guessed, I empathized, as I do with any lone thing forced outside humanity's confidences. I've never had to explain this, or any part of my nature to you, who lived outside for so long.

As it was, Kathleen and I regarded each other for the first time with clear access, her expression akin to that of a starving hunter prepping to disembowel a hare.

At home, we put everything we had into the other. When she came, tears basted her face.

I still felt distance.

Intarsia is a woodworking technique where various pieces of wood are fitted together to create an object or design. You can look things like that up. Other things you have to be born knowing.

I didn't tell Kathleen I consider touch to be the cheapest sense. I who have been punched, yanked across a room by my hair. Who've made what I thought was love with people who touched then left me with equal commitment, who never showed compassion through anything other than their fingertips.

Conversely, though my vision has always been poor, my eyes

have rarely betrayed me. When something smells wrong, it is. My hearing has been most loyal. Never anything anyone can hide in their voice. The sound of lying is an icicle cracking. The sound of wonder, release of pressure from a car jack.

Did you know that when a meteor passes Earth, it sizzles like bacon frying? That's how you sound to me.

In the final weeks, bronze arrived in Kathleen's tone as concrete built in mine.

We broke up at a culturally inappropriate gaucho café during the first storm of the summer. The final conversation was gentle. We were laminated in rain.

I had already bought the ticket for the trip that would bring me to your town, the street where you work, the restaurant where you liked to read on Sundays (until that point, alone), and where I first saw you through what felt like the opposite of glass. Dark skin, dark hair, dark eyes. You gave the candle I was born with something to do. Royal, flawed, and unforgiving. The facets in the gem finally turned in light's direction, and I flashed.

You are far away from me tonight yet hang in me like clothes on a line.

That night, I left the café, grateful and alone, and stepped outside where, to my dismay, it was no longer raining. Kathleen was already in sparkling conversation with the bartender, which made me glad. I saw her for a moment as he might, a beautiful woman in light colors, with nothing between her and the raging world.

# Every Forest, Every Film

◯

When I still lived in the city, I worked as a film critic for a poorly distributed, religiously read magazine and had gained a reputation for being overly critical. Hating everything was my entire personality, another reviewer wrote on their blog. I lived in a one-room apartment where for a design reason that remained unclear the toilet was in the middle of the living room. When a guest used it, I'd step onto the fire escape and listen to cars zing by. New York was thrilling and expensive and I spent most of every day feeling successful for staying alive.

One morning, in what would turn out to be my last month there, I awoke to a voice message from my father. He had sent a package and wanted to know if I'd received it. His usually calm voice was strained and he did not specify what the package contained. *Let me know. Received.* It must be important, I thought. Throughout the day I checked on breaks from writing a review about a new film that was highly touted for its use of idiosyncratic lighting ("clever but self-congratulatory") but could not rise above its lackluster performances ("stiff with self-regard").

My father did not answer his phone and no package arrived. Late in the afternoon, I made spaghetti with packet pesto, keeping the windows open so I could hear a late delivery. On the radio, pundits debated a proposed arms package. Planes flew overhead, filled with packages. Everything was a package.

The phone rang. I hoped it was my father but it was another

reviewer calling to see if I'd cover for her that night. She was supposed to see a show near the Navy Yard, in one of the yawning
expanses of lots, barbed wire, and distribution centers. I mostly
reviewed screeners and streaming television but she said this one
had to be in person.

The piece was called *The Cab*. Her tone implied that I should
know what it was and be grateful for the opportunity.

"If this film is so great, why aren't you taking it?"

"Show," she said. "Not film. You really haven't heard about it,
Milletti? Have you been out of the country?" She was the kind of
person who treated someone poorly while asking for a favor. I
admired her to the point of nausea. I loved that she used my last
name. Most people did; discreet groups from my life who didn't
know one another; friends from high school, coworkers. I have a
kind of expression or way of standing or speaking: People immediately considered me a teammate.

I told her I was as close as one could get to being out of the
country while being fully at home. I'd been in bed for the previous few days. She took it to mean I'd been having sex.

"Okay, girl, I see you." She sounded impressed.

"That's not what I'm saying."

She laughed as if I was being coy. "I see you."

One more thing about this person: Her name was Jude Law.
Like the actor. That's not significant, it's just a detail. Meaning it's
just as significant as anything else.

I'd been bedbound because I'd seen a photo online of my ex
at a wedding. He was wearing sunglasses and sitting next to a
woman with an elegant neck. I thought about the picture when I
soaped myself up in the shower then walked to the food store
where I debated what kind of mushrooms would keep their

integrity in the wok. I couldn't remember if he was wearing glasses and whether his hair was long or short so I looked at the photo again, and again was impressed by how little I cared so I crawled into bed and thought about the way his beard glimmered because even the sun favored him. The photo wore on me the way a river pummels stones.

I told Jude Law I'd take the job, anticipating gratitude but she said the tickets would be left at the counter and hung up.

The show took place in a warehouse that had been converted into a theater. After navigating a series of trains, I arrived sweating, gasping, and furious with myself that I had never strong-armed anyone into doing my job while acting aggravated. The warehouse, strung with purple lanterns, seems like a giant reproachful insect. There was no movie signage, yet a line of people stood outside. My curiosity clicked on. At that time, I was susceptible to a desire to be in on things.

Inside was a surprisingly new-looking lobby, awash in carpet. Even the counter was carpeted. It reminded me of the roller-skating rink from my youth. The bumpers and walls and tables were sheathed in plush so no one would get hurt if they fell. It made me sad to think about. In the winter of sixth grade, I skated alone to Whitney Houston's "So Emotional," thinking sad thoughts when my father, who'd arrived early to pick me up and had been watching from the side, yelled, "Hurry it up, Milletti, I'm not getting any younger!"

Even my father, who shared it and had given it to me, called me by my last name.

There was a mix-up with my ticket. Jude Law hadn't spoken to the right person or they'd misplaced it. This seemed to require several clerks to join the original clerk to search and talk. I left them arguing and went to the bathroom, lit by more purple lanterns. A woman standing near the door handed me a paper towel and when I thanked her, said, "I don't work here." She wore a vest buttoned over a turtleneck and official-looking joggers.

A text from my father read: DID THE PACKAGE ARRIVE?

I texted back: AM AT WORK WILL CHECK WHEN I GET HOME.

He texted a series of emojis that signified being grateful, in love, and horrified.

At the counter more clerks had joined the search for my ticket. One who seemed to command respect from the others announced, "This transaction was improperly handled from the start."

The original clerk looked panicked. My sympathy for workers battled my desire to go in and sit down. Finally, the respected clerk asked if it would be okay if I waited a few minutes. I told her that was fine, confused as to why it had taken so long to figure out when the answer had been a simple matter of a short delay.

I asked how the reception to the show had been so far.

"This is the first night," the original clerk said as the respected clerk said, "This is the only night."

This did not match Jude Law's attitude of surprised condescension upon my admission that I hadn't heard of this show. The matter settled, I took my ticket to a curtained wall and an usher emerged and said she would lead me to my cab. It was the vested woman from the bathroom.

"I thought you said you didn't work here."

"I said I didn't work there," she said, pointing toward the bathrooms.

She held back a section of curtain and I passed into a country-dark vacuous space that felt mammoth. The stark contrast of moving from the lobby to this space made me pause to collect my bearings. I sensed large structures hulking in the darkness and people milling about. My eyes adjusted and I realized they were cabs, larger than any I'd seen, with a few rows of seats inside. The line of them seemed to extend for miles.

"What kind of trick is this?" I asked the woman.

She did not reply but guided me to her vehicle, which had an enormous windshield that shone in errant light. Smaller, diamond-shaped portholes dotted the sides. She slid open the wide door, startling a couple inside, who gathered their belongings. The driver allowed them to pass then gestured for me to take a seat. I chose the back row. I liked to have a buffering distance between me and whatever I was considering. The driver closed the door and lights went up inside the vehicle as if it were a theater. She took her seat up front. A partition between us ascended as she arranged her legs around the steering wheel. I peered out one of the portholes, obscured by city muck, but could no longer see the warehouse. The "cab" lurched forward. The sensation of movement was uncanny. Through the windshield, I could see we were driving through a city I didn't recognize. The Eiffel Tower. The Space Needle. Paris and Seattle? Explosions fireworked over the horizon. We passed a large power plant I strained to see through the windows.

My pulse quickened. Important, surprising works were rare. "This is very realistic!" I called up to her. She pointed to her ears and shook her head.

She turned onto a road that spiraled up a steep hill. The

switchbacks were narrow but I remembered a story about how bus drivers in the Andes mountains knew their roads as if the routes were imprinted in their bodies. I glimpsed sharp cliffs and reminded myself we were still inside a theater. As if to test my conviction, the cab skittered on a patch of loose gravel. She pumped the brake as the back wheel flirted with the treacherous drop-off. I made a noise of shock, an "awl" triggered by real fear. The illusion was whole, the driver did a masterful job of feigning this momentary lapse of control. The cab halted and we took a few long breaths. A hawk screeched above the cab, its call bouncing off the vast space of a canyon. The driver pressed the accelerator and we moved around the curve.

We traveled the road for several minutes as I attempted to figure out our destination. Authentic-feeling desert air crept into the cab. I shook off my sweater, my back dotted with sweat.

We passed a roadside bodega. A man sat outside, smoking. I made a gesture of salutation to him that he, impossibly, returned. Every so often the driver pulled off to the side so another "cab" could pass. I couldn't deduce how they were executing the lighting, timing, and movement.

"When does the show start?"

She sped toward another sharp curve at the end of the road. The velocity pressed me into my seat, halted my breath. She accelerated. I assumed she'd slow at the last moment in the expert way years of experience had taught her. Instead, she barreled faster toward it. We could not make it around. I cried out.

We launched over the ledge. My stomach lifted. I clutched the arm of the seat, anticipating the drop. But instead of falling we hovered above a valley of terra-cotta homes with lush, complicated gardens. The buoyancy of sudden elevation spread through my stomach as we climbed. My ears popped as we flew over the valley. I had never seen homes as gentle and singular, like those I'd read about in childhood fantasy novels. Owls and turquoise doors and wildflower gardens. Cottages tucked into hollows, laden with moss. A woman wearing a red dress knelt in the middle of a field of cabbages so healthy they seemed sentient. Complex and green. Happiness, I thought, swiping a tear from my cheek. But why would this prompt emotion?

We flew toward an expanse of navy mountains outlined in the dying sun. Their darkness grew as we approached. Homes blinked throughout the foothills, cars snaked up tiny roads. My driver accelerated. Trees and more homes in the ridges. We were near enough to see a lean, muscled girl standing in a driveway. She waved us away, we were too close. Her voice reached us in the cab. "Go back," she called. Again, my body reacted as if we were going to crash. I yelled, "No!" And, "Hey!" The cabbie ignored me. I covered my eyes. Trees filled the ridges and we slammed against the side.

At impact, the lights came up. The walls of the vehicle had vanished. I found myself in a room of seating arrangements being manned by their own drivers, dressed similarly in vests and joggers, though the cabs were gone. Dazed audience members gathered their belongings. Others arrived. I realized I was in the middle of a structure that had many beginnings. But that wasn't the whole of it. When people arrived, the cab cars sprang up around them and flew away. I could see landscapes through the departing windshields that were different from the one I'd traveled through. Forests, tropical islands, cityscapes. But this would imply infinite shows. Did the drivers have a route or was it a surprise for them too? The sensation of hitting the mountain coursed through my body. I was only beginning to understand what I had experienced.

I left my section, found the curtained wall, and stumbled across the lobby. Disoriented, I tripped on a fold in the carpet and landed on my knees. The contents of my purse spilled across the floor. Hair ties, coins, and lemon chews launched away from me with force, as if fleeing. I hadn't realized how many items I'd been carrying. A woman stepped around the items as if I had vomited. I attempted to gather the mess, but items evaded my wide reach. I embraced the ground again and again. A group of formally dressed men approached and asked how much certain items were. They held up my tampons, date book, the banana I carried in case someone went into diabetic shock, the bookmark my ex gave me, my glasses case.

"They're not for sale." I shooed them, pain blooming in my forehead. Something about the show had dug a nail into me. I didn't want to interact. I wanted to go home and get back into bed and after taking five trains that's what I did. No package had come while I'd been out. I texted my father THE PACKAGE FAILED TO SHOW, which felt appropriately dramatic.

In uneasy dreams a package waited for me to arrive. I was on my way, but I was late.

At sunrise, I did not stay in bed like I had every other morning. I took the stairs to the sidewalk and walked into the middle of the street. Even New York City is quiet and carless at 7:00 a.m. I turned to the east as if it might yield a courier. I turned to the west.

Inside, my phone was ringing. It was my father.

"Never mind," he said. "Your mother never took it to the post office. We're taking it later today."

"What is it?" I said. "What is the package?"

"Your high school tennis trophy. We thought you'd want it. Now that you no longer have a husband. To remind you: you were once at the top of your game."

"My high school trophy? But that's not important! Why were you making it sound urgent?"

In the moment that passed I heard a plane climb to cruising altitude.

"Sometimes," my father said, "I don't know how to talk to you."

That afternoon, I wrote and filed a rare positive review ("Inspired soundscape. Terrifyingly real"), but I was coming to the end of something. I'd grown weary of seeking new sentiment for what was normally conventional and routine. *The Cab* underlined a disappointment I'd been harboring: Every film follows the same beats. I wasn't overly critical, I only longed for innovation. This desire compounded a feeling that an important central force in the city that once loved me was now indifferent. And how far we all were from the forest. We had approximations of it corralled into parks, but they only proved how far away we were from the actual actual. I realized: they're tricking us. My clothes felt so heavy I feared I'd collapse. I imagined myself at age ninety on a fire escape, trying to block the sound of flushing.

I moved as north as one can while still being in the city limits, then farther, into the silent, restless woods. I can't be the first to say it: A forest is a verb. Whether you're in one seems based on whether you're somewhere or only on the verge of somewhere. Something regularly shifts out of sight. I like it: I keep moving, too. I am always ever-so-slightly beyond my reach.

When did you cut your hair?

# In the Basement of Saint John
the Divine

○

Though they can't see much in the basement of Saint John the Divine, the boys know, with the peculiar insight of those who wish to do harm, where the other boy is, dreaming in his sleeping bag so new the red is bright, so new the zipper sticks. James. They hate this boy and his bag because, among other reasons, so-new-the-zipper-sticks means he's never slept earth-prone in nature's wildness, as boys must. Rows of sleeping bags cover the basketball court in the dimly lit crypt. Here and there the boys step over a king or queen clutching a tinfoil scepter.

James still does not see in dreams but hears what Spider-Man hears—the door's creak in the third comic frame. The clack of shoes when the evil doctor enters. Spider-Man senses the doctor's shadow climb him where he sits, chained to a safe. Dreaming, James makes a tiny fist.

He wakes with the hands of other boys on him. Two of them, brothers, hold his struggling shoulders under the lip of the bag, while the other cinches and winds its cord. The boys are silent—they've discussed this—and professionally rough. James maintains a chattering laugh so they won't think he's a bad sport if it turns out to be a joke.

"Quiet." They are disappointed in him. "You wanna wake everyone up?"

Even in distress, James knows by the transitive property of

suffering that summoning the Head Knight would go double bad for him.

"Please be patient. I used to be blind." The phrase doesn't quite fit, but it's all he's practiced.

The boys consult one another with quick glances. Is he the dumbest kid alive? The largest boy's tone is almost kind: "We know."

A floor above, the cathedral's nave soars higher than the Statue of Liberty. Finished, the boys check the knots, affirming the fit so he can breathe but not move. James is trapped from the neck down. The soft fabric digs into his Adam's apple, cutting off air if he struggles. "Let me go."

His plaintiveness disgusts them. Same goes for the tears that glimmer when he looks toward the crypt, where earlier he'd heard the chaperones, his father among them, shuffling cards.

One of the boys guesses his intent. "Don't even think about it."

James's bare desire to be liked is not the correct way to participate. He should toss his head, *no big deal*, but it's hard to act aloof when confined, even for James, who had feigned compliance in their snide remarks throughout the day, going so far as pitching in to insult himself. The boys' disgust shifts to boredom. They leave him wriggling inside the satiny bag and congratulate one another with blows to the elbows and hips. James lies back on the ground. He is the trunk of a tree that stands on a meadow. Above him his branches revolve, pleating, pinking, diamonding the sun's light.


Knightwatch had been a hard sell for James's father, Edward, who read the brochure aloud while he and Keisha brushed their teeth:

*Imaginative experiences in the Gothic cathedral. Children will be transported to the medieval age of jesters, princesses, and knights.*

Keisha and James share an indention in their right cheek—the size and shape of a fingernail clipping—that appears when they are feeling skeptical. This eclipse of faith happening daily as Edward suggested activities that until then had been impossible. Solo store trips, Friday-night comedy sets, allowing James to sleep in a bag surrounded by children dressed as courtesans. Almost two years had passed since the tree with lights and James spent only a few days each month wearing the blindfold. The dark a guilty, pressing comfort.

Keisha still said no.

Edward adopted a conversational tone, as if he'd just heard exciting news. "Peacocks roam the grounds."

They'd been sitting in quiet, eating cereal and reading newspapers. Keisha turned her attention from one side of the newspaper to the other. "Peacocks?"

"Peacocks," he said, driving the boy to school.

Thinking it might bear a collective effect on his wife, he proselytized more broadly, telling everyone.

"Foam practice swords!" to the crossing guard.

"Across from Tom's Diner," to his office's receptionist.

"Tom's Diner," he reminded a colleague, "is famous."

"Clay gargoyles!" he yelped at her parents' house.

"What's he talking about?" Keisha's mother said.

"Some Camelot thing." The fingernail fleck from Keisha.

"There's a tightrope walker in residence for Christ's sake." He pounded his steering wheel, alone in the car, sent out for some forgotten sauce. Stopped at a red light, around him unending meadow lit by a disapproving moon. "Jousting," he told it.

In the end, jealousy convinced her: Her former comedy partner—the one who warned her that kids would sink her career—scored a sitcom. The one who said they should move away from observational comedy because young comics were going weird. Knightwatch lined up with an opening at her old club. This was Keisha's chance to return to the stage, a counterbalance to her days at the dentist's office, showing disbelieving teens Plasticine versions of future bites. He would take care of the boy, and she would be too distracted by nerves to worry about them.

They bought James a sleeping bag, a backpack, a starter Dopp Kit. They traced a sword on a cardboard box. Edward had provided his family an opportunity to grow and it was already manifesting in props. What was this catch at the base of his throat, watching the boy hunched over his work? Pride.


All morning they searched for peacocks.

Edward followed James around every corner, the kid always certain he'd glimpsed a plume of sharp feathers. The cathedral had so many corners to imagine something great behind. James pointed to the next, the next, but around each one, no peacock.

At noon they joined the others and climbed the highest spire to observe the bones and sinews. "A weep hole permits a flow of air that prevents condensation," a guide explained.

The tour paused in an eave where the tightrope walker kept his studio. They were not permitted to enter, but Edward allowed James to peek after the rest had moved on.

"A bed and a desk with books!" James reported.

"What's he reading?" Edward said.

"I didn't see."

"Go look!"

James returned a moment later. "It's a porno!"

Edward's laughter echoed over the terraces, prompting the last members of the tour, two dour girls strapped diagonally by identical satchels, to turn and glare. Edward descended the spiral staircase behind his son. The stone walls yellowed by time. The back of James's head in the eggy light. A fraction of knuckle on the ancient banister. As they wound down, James disappeared again and again.

"Lollipop," the guide said when they reached the ground. "Buttress." She gestured to the nave, the height of the Statue of Liberty. "Oculi. Rib and pier." James lifted his gaze along with the other children and, with the other children, counted each one.

In the chancel, a tightrope stretched taut between the walls, shoulder high.

"A practice wire," the guide said.

Lollipop. Oculi. These new words matched Edward's feeling as if, instead of the infrastructure, his vaulting fatherhood was being detailed. Rib and pier. The way James raised his hand to ask, "What makes a cathedral Gothic?"

"Three elements," the guide said. "Majestic dimensions, soaring verticality, and structural clarity. They build the cathedral's frame in wood then encase it in stone. After the stone sets, they incinerate the wooden skeleton and hope the exterior holds."

Edward imagined a sputtering line of fire spreading over an expansive scaffolding.

After lunch, the students were divided into groups and given practice swords. They thrusted and parried across the floor, wearing brightly colored felt vestments. Dinner was preprepared salads and chicken grilled in the atrium. The sound of children scooping corn and rice from metal bowls.

After dinner, Edward lifted James so he could report over a courtyard wall: a garden, peacockless. The birds were no-shows and didn't matter. What did: When had Edward and his boy ever been in on something? Before surgery (they never said when James was blind), he'd pout if Edward attempted to guide him.

The children unrolled their sleeping bags on the basement floor. The Head Knight, a regional-theater actor, stood on the three-point line and told a story about a dragon.

Even before friends averted their gazes, before their refusal to send him away to "blind kid camp," a scrim had been yanked between him and Keisha. It had been so long since they'd shared love's telepathy, he saw her as if from the other side of a lake. They didn't talk but signaled. Edward's need for human contact became primal. He'd had sex a few times with a colleague. She let him come inside of her. This seemed to be a big deal to men he'd heard all his life overtalking at the gym. After a month, the thrill of her skin migrated to his stomach and turned to rot. He'd stepped into the cathedral one afternoon wanting to feel redeemable. That's when he saw the flyer for Knightwatch.

Whatever state his marriage was in, the sleepover had worked. Their boy had thrusted and parried and spoken up. Regular as bread.

In the basement of Saint John the Divine, Edward experienced a wealth of feeling.

It's over, he thought. We made it.

———

The Head Knight and the other chaperones play rummy in the crypt, slapping down aces with mock seriousness and sneaking slips of liquor from a flask. Edward strolls the lines of sleeping bags, promising himself he's not checking on James. Sleeping children press the things they love against their cheeks. He stoops to replace a princess's fallen wand.

He reaches James's group and registers something wrong with the scene immediately.

James is not asleep but struggling. His shoulders batter against the stubborn bag.


Edward, James, and the boys sit in the crypt while the Head Knight paces.

"I'm going to ask again," he says. "Did you tie James up in his sleeping bag?"

The boys jostle on their folding chairs.

"Isaac?" The Head Knight correctly identifies the leader, Edward thinks, by his brutish body already bearing a man's love handles.

Isaac says it was a joke and the other boys nod. "Sorry if the kid can't take a joke."

"A joke," the Head Knight says. It's not possible he's falling for this classic bully response. Can't take a joke? The kid's goddamned mother is a comedian. But the Head Knight turns to James, eyes merry with relief, asking if he may have misunderstood.

James stares out the door toward the basketball court built, they learned, because the monks love basketball. It will be up to him to return everyone to their sleeping bags and card games.

Edward prays that James has inherited his mother's relentless ability to question. Every detail about the surgery, every medication and side effect.

"Yes," James says. "A joke."

Isaac, already sliding off his chair, expecting absolution.

"Not so fast," the Head Knight says, relieved. "Apologize to James."

"Sorry," the boys mumble. Edward watches them leave, affecting warrior postures as soon as the Head Knight rejoins his cards. James's expression as he follows them makes it clear he thinks Edward should have intervened. Shame heats his neck, his vaulting fatherhood is collapsing. He must do something.

"James." The volume echoes against the old walls, compelling even the doltish boys to halt.


At first, we reach for what is near.

Edward and Keisha taught James the world by touch beginning with the items in their apartment. This is what a dry sponge feels like. A wet. This is a loaf of bread. A single slice. A made bed. Unmade. Feel and taste the letter $M$. Touch the desk. Daddy's stubble. Mommy's hair.

They varied their tones during feeding, dressing, diapering so he could know his situation by sound. They narrated every action: I am placing the fork next to the knife. I am folding the napkin. James rested his hands on theirs and they guided him. Hand under hand. Hand over hand. Soon, Edward described his actions even when James wasn't present, felt the tender weight of his son's palms as he drove his car.

What does noon sound like? A garden? They figured out

sound cues for every human situation. For day shifting into night, parents in the suburbs could teach their sightless children to listen for crickets, but there are no crickets in Queens. The meat cart vendors scraping their carts home at end of day were all James had. If their friends could do better, let them deal with the tripling of parental helplessness.

James never resented blindness but could not forgive them for sight. The assault of light. That gigantic mess with the tree. He did not understand that objects in the distance were not actually smaller. If a lamp occludes the curtain, the lamp is closer. Over time, he didn't need them to explain when it was dusk because he could see it. He moved his new eyes over Edward and Keisha, comparing them to other objects, relaying information to his brain about their bodies' positions around the house, around one another. The distance between Keisha and him. If Daddy occludes Mommy, Daddy is closer.

James longed for his friends at his old school, some of whose parents no longer considered Edward and Keisha part of the group. "You make a mistake when you think of sight as a cure," one kindly explained. If a challenge arose when they weren't there, they taught James to say: Please be patient. I just regained my sight. That he no longer needed their help left them with a criminal thought of parenthood: If their son no longer needed them, who were they? Keisha took it hard, but Edward was thrilled. The world that had never changed anything to accommodate his sightless son now seemed to open like a rose.

From their booth across the street, James and his father can see the full span of the cathedral, its spires scribbled against the night sky, but James is more interested in his milkshake. The blend of vanilla and ice and the thrill of the late hour nullifies his anger at the Head Knight, the boys, and his father, who places his phone on the table between them. "Let's call your mother."

"What will we tell her?"

"The truth, of course." His father's voice wobbles on the word.

Her tone is curt when she answers, his father had been expected to call much earlier. James hears noise behind her.

His father checks his watch. "Still at the club?"

"I figured one drink wouldn't hurt. I've been waiting to hear from you," she reminds him.

"You're on speaker," his father says.

Her voice becomes pleasant. "Hi, little boy."

"Hi, Mom."

"Your grand return to the stage," his father says. "How did it go?"

A clink of gruff talking.

"Honey?"

"Great," she says. "Like no time had passed. The owner said he couldn't believe it."

Acknowledgment swivels between father and son: she's lying.

"How is it going there? Please tell me. I've been thinking about you guys all night."

Outside, a couple walks by clutching a single dark coat around them. James and his father exchange a glance.

"Couldn't be better," his father says at the same time James says, "So much fun!"

"Thank god," she says.

When the updates are over, his parents talk freely. His mother shares a few of what she calls "child appropriate" jokes from the night. His father listens, one side of his mouth already lifted, anticipating the laugh.

Later, a fluttering in the periphery of his dreams. James awakens in the darkness of the basketball court, unsure whether it's morning or night. The basement smells like steak and the armpits of teenagers. He worms out of his bag. In the chamber attached to the crypt, cards are fanned in their final hands.

Stone saints and plaster gargoyles rest in storage near the back staircase. James climbs to the corridor with enormous windows that runs alongside the cathedral. The gray of the statues lightens and the heads of the tulips rise, indicating a shift from night to day. Near a corner garden, a peacock shuffles in place. For a moment, James does not believe in it. It is a phantasm or a trick of imagination. But real enough to squawk so James can hear it. The peacock is plainer than James expected. A dirty swan with a graceful mohawk. But its aliveness is palpable, as if it could move through the window that separates them without disturbing the glass. It beaks its wings, its pale train performing a kind of hypnosis. James stares until he forgets that the bird is a form made of light and atoms, controlled by synapses and impulses from a main generator in its tiny head. That he is too.

The doctors said a tree was a bad idea.

Unfiltered light can traumatize the newly sighted. Some children beg to return to darkness. After surgery, James would have to wear a blindfold until his eyes built frames to corral tincture and hue.

When the blindfold was removed would depend on how quickly James's eyes learned to protect themselves, that's how his parents explained it.

After a month, the doctors asked James what he'd like to see first.

"A tree," he said.

Too many stimuli, the doctors said, from too many sources, but for once his parents insisted.

They drove to a field outside the city at dusk when light would be dulled. He'd be the one to take off the blindfold—he stated this several times on the drive. They sat on the grass drinking sodas out of cans. His father said an interesting thing happened in the office that week but couldn't remember the important detail that made it a story and not just a collection of events. James announced he was ready, but when they counted to three he couldn't do it. They counted to three again.

His mother described the tree that stood at the edge of the pond. It had several trunks growing out of its base. Some of the trunks were very thick. His mother said the sun was sinking behind the multi-trunked tree, casting an orange glow on the pond. "When you open your eyes, you'll see the color orange on the water. Orange is the color of citrus fruit. The trunks will be dark gray. Gray is the color of a pigeon or the sky before a storm. The grass will be dark green in the places the sun has dried. The sun has outlined the tree in pale yellow. The colors grow into deeper shades of themselves every minute." His mother said, "It doesn't have to happen today. It can happen next week, or even next year."

"Honey," his father warned.

"Know what?" she said. "It's his goddamned life."

"I'm ready." James slid the blindfold off and placed it on the blanket beside him. He sat for a moment with his eyes closed. "No countdown."

"Take it slow," his father said.

"No rush," his mother said.

James opened his eyes and tried to focus on the tree. Its colors battered him like noise. He didn't want to fail. He blinked and blinked, dissolving against his father's side as his mother reached to steady him. James closed his eyes. This went beyond what he could muffle. His parents covered him with a blanket as if he were on fire, carried him weeping to the car, and sped away like the field itself had done the damage.

A creak from inside the cathedral startles James and the peacock, who shivers and reveals plumage. The fanfare is so pale it appears translucent, and is concave, James sees, as the bird walks toward him. Each feather is crowned by a precise V, as if the peacock carries a migration of attendant birds. Not at all like a dirty swan! Less sparrow, more velociraptor.

James hears a shuffling inside the cathedral. He leaves the peacock and enters the chamber. A man is balanced on the practice wire in the chancel. He reads a paperback and sings. French, James thinks, hiding in one of the bays.

The man toes the air and flips a page. He switches feet, dips with the other foot. Flips a page.

The sun has crept into the upper choir lofts but where the man balances remains in shadow. It takes James several minutes to realize the man is staring at him.

"Well?" the man says.

"Hello." James walks the long aisle to the altar. "I'm James."

"Hello, James." The man uses his weight to make the wire dip. "You're one of the knights."

James remembers the felt vestment he wears over his pajamas.

The man disembarks from the wire as if stepping from a curb. He closes the book and lays it on the altar. Muscles are visible through his pants and T-shirt as he takes the two steps down to where James stands. He moves with feline dignity, covering more ground than he should in a short amount of time.

He motions to the wire. "You'll try."

"No," James says, but the man takes his hand and leads him to the chair. Forgoing it, he lifts James to the ledge with ease.

"Step onto the wire," he says. "Look forward, not at the ground or at me. Don't let go of my hand."

The wire is wider than James could see from the ground, three or so inches, which means the odds of balancing are greater than he thought. He tests it with his foot. It feels unfriendly, which cheers him because he does not want what holds him to be finicky. When he shifts weight to his foot, he is confronted by fear.

"Good," the man says. "You know what it is."

James leans forward, one foot still on the safety of the ledge.

"Look in front of you, not down." His hand is thin like James's mother's but stronger. James moves his second foot onto the wire. The realization that he is supported by nothing startles him and he retreats to the ledge.

The man's expression is grim. "That will teach you to think."

James places one foot then the other on the wire.

"Now walk."

James considers and dismisses lying. "I'm afraid I'll fall."

"You won't," the man says. "I have you."

His tone expects compliance. James doesn't think even Isaac could mess with this man, who gestures to indicate impatience.

"Look forward not down," the man says.

James steps away from the safety of the ledge. There is no longer anything underneath him. He takes another step.

"Bounce," the man says. "Gently."

James uses his weight to make the wire dip.

"Good," the man says. "Now, close your eyes."

Panic tightens James's chest. He has misjudged the man, he is not cool with talent, but a bully like Isaac and his friends. He has led him out here to fail and fall. He should've stayed in the basement, dreaming of Spider-Man.

The man waits. James battles himself on the wire.

"I can't," he says finally. "This is far enough."

"Close your eyes." The man's volume increases around the command. "I have you."

James remembers a detail from the tour. "The first rule of a building," the guide said, "is to not fall down." His father had repeated this and other phrases. James had found this annoying but is grateful because he knows that the flying buttresses deliver their counterthrusts into the walls. This conveys the lateral force that pushes the walls away from the building, divvying the unseen pressure down a granite column to the ground. James hears in his father's voice: *The walls do not carry the weight of the roof.* It calms him.

"What if I fall?" he says.

The man says, "You won't."

The last thing James sees before he closes his eyes: a statue of a winged girl on the opposite wall, her porcelain face lifted to some benevolent, troubling force that hovers above her, above him.

# Flowers and Their Meanings

◯

The summer my mother has hernia surgery, a tiger escapes from our tiny shore-town zoo.

I'm eighteen, wear shirts tied in the back with shoelaces, and my ringtone is "Houses of the Holy." When I pick my mother up from the hospital, the nurses stand in a line to hug her goodbye.

"I have that effect," she tells me.

For three months she cannot lift anything heavier than a sack of flour. My responsibilities include lowering her into and helping her out of various chairs, beds, and baths, watering her zinnias, and driving her to the town library to look for the next volume in her crime series. I'm in a new relationship with ice bags, hoses, murder, and sandwiches. Every afternoon I prepare the latter based on that day's desires.

Her initial discomfort at accepting help quickly switches to a tendency to bark orders. "Avocado!" she yells from the bath. "Lettuce!" while I am snipping off the heads of dead zinnias. "Iceberg! Not the thin stuff." Sometimes she demands a pickle, sometimes gets annoyed I'd even offer a pickle. Sometimes a thick layer of mayonnaise.

Each book in her murder series is titled for a letter from the alphabet. *A Is for Arrest Me, B Is for Bronchitis, C Is for Come Here, Brian* . . . The library anchors the strip mall with our Chinese food restaurant and the pharmacy, where I compare earnest sunglasses in the moon-shaped mirror while she scours the stacks.

The library usually does not have the letter she needs and she leaves empty-handed and morose. Although each volume re-introduces every character, including the heroine, my mother insists on reading them in order. She enjoys proper procedure and doesn't want to hear my theories about narrative memory.

One day, the library has the right volume. Rejoining me in the pharmacy, she brandishes the glossy book and declares, "*H Is for Homicide*!"

We drive home and I lower her into the recliner. All she wants to do is read. Still, I collect activity pamphlets from the pharmacy.

"Mah-jongg," I say. "Mom-jong."

She does not look up from her book. "Fools play card games."

"The zoo?"

She flips a page. "It doesn't even have a tiger."

I hold up the zoo pamphlet. On the cover, a tiger roars.

"Well, anyway, not a very good one. I don't like to see them caged. Standing there. Wondering, what on earth am I doing here?"

I work in the Women's Clothing section in Mandee's, usually with Joan, another local girl, whose gentle voice masks an almost debilitating anxiety. *Like the big-time chains, but hometown,* Mandee's jingle hopes. The store is in a converted warehouse with clumsy carpets and dividers to set off departments. Mandee from Mandee's insists we work in teams—the home-goods team, the electronics team. Joan and I are the afternoon shift of the ready-to-wear team. During our training we learned that a greeted customer is less likely to steal. We're supposed to say hello to everyone even if they are cutting through our section to get to Pets, even if we have already greeted them. It's as important as checking the dressing rooms at the end of the day to make sure no one's hiding, Mandee says. Once, Mandee says, a ready-to-wear employee startled a man who'd been sleeping there. Every night, he'd scoot in before close and wait under a display until everyone left. He'd borrow a pillow and blanket from Housewares and sleep in the dressing room for people with special needs.

"We can't have people sleeping in ready-to-wear," Mandee says.

During our training, Joan asked Mandee if a team could be only two people and she answered, "Can a family be two people?" which was more progressive than I anticipated from the owner of a store that had separate break rooms for men and women.

As if the tiger has heard my mother bemoan its captivity, it escapes. The newscasters make jokes. *Wants to get started on its tan, getting a jump on summer sales.* The timing is uncanny. Has my mother's thought somehow freed this tiger? Joan and I watch the coverage on our phones. Kindergartens and grade schools close early. The hotline is flooded with tips. "I saw it go into the Pine Barrens," one woman says, pointing a trembling finger off camera.

My mother ignored the hernia for three years until it grew to the size of a baseball. Whenever it emerged, she'd massage it until it receded. The final time, she lay on the couch unable to move for hours until she, on the brink of unconsciousness, relented to the pain and called me.

"*S* is for stubborn," I tell her.

She says, "*P* is for pain-in-the-neck daughters."

One afternoon after the tiger escapes, I'm walking a two-lane highway looking for shade and admiring the street names, thinking I'd like to live on one named Violet when a truck slows next to me and its driver leans out the window to ask if I want to watch him masturbate. The truck seems new, oversize. The street is basted in heat. Like every other man in this salted-stiff bay town, he wears satiny basketball shorts (pushed down mid-thigh) and could be anywhere from twenty to fifty. He tugs his soft flesh, already doing it.

I rescind the step I'd taken toward him when I assumed he was asking directions or the time. The noise I make sounds like no.

"Your loss." He pulls away.

A sprinkler gyrates across a nearby lawn. Dust pillows out from the retreating truck.

The reason I'm walking has to do with my friend's boyfriend getting arrested. She and her two kids needed to go to the police station, where the boyfriend left their truck. My mother's van is loaned to a friend running errands. Everyone's car is in the wrong place. I'm walking to my friend's house to drive her neighbor's car to the station.

At the house, my friend's daughters stare out the screen door like mournful, landlocked mariners. I follow their gazes down the road to where the truck slowed, beyond the erratic, dust-filled breeze, beyond the bay roiling with crabs. Whatever the boyfriend did has scared them polite. DUI, it turns out, his second or third. My friend tells me he'll spend a few nights in jail.

I don't know much about kids, but I know you're supposed to protect them from adult idiocy. I twirl the neighbor's keys and pretend to holster them on my hip like a gun. "Off we go," I say.

The girls look at their mom to gauge whether they can laugh. Her eyes remind me of the sunbaked road I'd taken there— nowhere to hide. She says, "Don't make that asshole a game."


The boyfriend looks sheepish, like instead of going to jail he is about to ask my friend to go to prom. He holds out his hands as you'd cradle a hat but there are just two leaping kids and an angry woman I knew in high school. I'd gotten back in touch with her in a rare gesture of nostalgic optimism I was every day regretting.

As they talk, I play a game with the girls that I call "What will you do with me?" "Imagine I'm made out of rose petals," I say.

"I'll pluck you," the oldest says, and the younger, "I'll throw you down at a wedding."

I hear the boyfriend say, *There's no way of knowing.* Her flat reply, *Yes, there is,* seems to cue the sun that hurries through the window and turns everything edgeless until the room seems like a cliff I can fall from.

"Imagine I'm made out of syrup," one of the girls says.

"I'll put you on waffles," the other says.

I say, "I'll marinate kielbasa in you."

The boyfriend drove me home once. During the ride, he pretended to hit certain people on the street then assigned himself points. Two points for an old man, three points for a VW Beetle. The sheer energy required to maintain something like that. Most people engage in games as a pleasant way to pass time, but when he dropped me at my mother's house, he remembered the tally. They should have arrested him for that, I'm thinking, when my friend says in a big voice that she's ready to leave.

One cricket-thick July evening, Joan finds me, folding bralettes into a pile that pleases me.

"Someone's stuck," she says.

"Stuck where?"

"Not where," she says. "In."

"Hello," I say to a passing customer, startling her. "In what?"

"A dress, I think. One of those long ones I can never remember the name for."

I follow her to the dressing room where a woman stands in the common area, arms up, stuck inside a yellow floral maxi dress. She waves, yelping softly.

I introduce myself and ask if she minds if I try the zipper.

"Try anything," she says.

The zipper refuses to move and the excess folds meant to billow are cinched around her torso and breasts. The cheap fabric won't negotiate. The more she struggles, the more stuck she becomes.

"It's like cloth quicksand," Joan says.

"Ma'am, please stop moving." I inform Joan we will have to cut the woman out and ask her to borrow a pair of shears from Garden and Home.

Joan leaves. I hear her helloing customers as she crosses the retail floor.

I guide the woman into a sitting position on the ottoman and attempt chat. She is an independent contractor working on the new resort but they closed early because everyone is scared about the tiger, so she came in to try on what she calls "one of those flowy dresses everyone is wearing." "They are not flattering for those of us with a chest."

"They're not for everyone," I agree.

"Do you think that tiger is okay?" Her voice is tight, sad.

"Well, if it made it to the Pine Barrens, I'm sure it's fine. Nothing gets out of there."

"What an idiot I am." She shakes with what I think is laughter but turns out to be crying. I place my hand near where I hope is her shoulder.

She wears beige no-show socks. The slip of the dress covers her thighs, her arms are fixed above her head. It would appear to anyone passing that I am talking to a wind sock, or some day lily come to life. Joan returns with the shears.

I pull the fabric away from the stuck woman's skin and Joan cuts. The woman is silent as we slice through the dress. When we are almost finished, the zipper admits defeat and relents the rest of the way. The woman emerges and turns out to be white, middle aged, with a wide, smooth face. After a few shaky steps around the room, she slips into her old dress, thanks us, and leaves.

We tell each other the story for the rest of the shift. How Joan found her, flailing in the room. How I made conversation while Joan got the shears. The fabric strips, peeling away.

"I thought she was going to look different," I say.

Joan nods. "Anyone could have been under there."

A woman in the doorway holds up two pocketbooks and wants to know the difference between cognac and brown.

Joan says, "One's darker."


When my mother called me to admit she'd been enabling a hernia for three years, she was gasping through pain.

By the time I reached the house, she'd passed out. That was the first time I felt her cool limbs slinking away from my grip, been that close to her powdery smell. The doctors said if she'd waited any longer the hernia would have ruptured. They told me this after the surgery when my mother was safe. But during a moment at the house when she was so supremely uncarryable, I did not think I could do it. I sank to the ground with her in my arms. I knew she would die and I was ready to shoulder that blame instead of proceeding. Her body seemed comprised of hundreds of independently operating parts. It has to end, anyway, I thought, ready to surrender to the unfairness, which would in some way be a relief. It was late afternoon. The seagulls were screaming. Who was I to deserve relief? I stumbled and pulled and dragged our way to the car. I drove and pounded the steering wheel and backhanded tears from my eyes so I could see all the way to the Regional Hospital where they removed a baseball from my mother's stomach and I ate a wilted sandwich from the commissary and watched her dot on the electric board remain blue—in crisis, in crisis, in crisis, and just when I was convinced a doctor would appear at any moment to break the news and I was braced and taut and in agony, it changed to orange, in recovery.

I yank the heavy hose around the garden while my mother points out the thirstiest plants.

On a tall zinnia, I notice a long-limbed and delicate bug.

"Look." I point. "A praying mantis."

"That's your father," my mother says. "I'd know that look of disgust anywhere. Hey, Tony."

"Praying mantises are female," I say, not certain.

"Not one doubt." My mother turns the hose on him. The praying mantis moves farther up the stem like an elegant afterthought. Like he has done this with her a million times.

Later, I deliver her a veggie burger with avocado and lettuce sliced on the diagonal and instead of taking a bite she gazes at it. "Now that's a heartbreaking sandwich," she says.

"What makes it heartbreaking?"

She raises her arms as if in disgust. "Look at it!"

The tiger evades capture for weeks. Lore spreads. It is looking for its lover from whom it was brutally separated when it came to this town. The tiger has been heartbroken for years and this is a lover's daring stunt to be reunited.

———

It is a good day for my mother and the library. She emerges with *N Is for Noose* and a book called *Flowers and Their Meanings*. She reads from it as I drive.

"'A yellow rose means infidelity and disloyalty. A pink carnation is *I will never forget you*. *Be mine* is clover. *My heart burns* is cactus.'"

That night, I water the *thoughts of absent friends* and think, I don't want to end up like the heroine in my mother's murder series, perpetually surprised by her town's crappy tendencies.

"Whoever did this must really hate women," she says nearly every time.

If I were a writer, I'd give her an accomplice like Joan, who would say something like *It's as if you could have guessed that from literally every fucking case we've worked together.*

It's a good joke. I laugh while watering *cure*, *maternal error*, and *no*! As if to reward my clever thought, the praying mantis appears, stares at me from the side of his carapace, testing one ridiculous leg then the other. I'm not sure it's my father, but I wouldn't rule out that it's someone's.

At the end of summer, the ready-to-wear team has inventory night. Every other team goes home at close of day but Joan and I count tanks and camis. The warehouse is dark except for our section. We finish at midnight and Joan checks the dressing and break rooms. When she returns, she's trembling. "There's someone in the women's break room. Some thing. An animal."

I don't know why my first thought is bat but, "Bat?" I say.

"Way bigger. It's the lion," she says. "Wait. What's the one with the mane?"

I tell her lion is the one with the mane and she says then it's the tiger.

"Tigers have stripes," I check.

"It has stripes," she says.

It has only been a few weeks since the woman was trapped in the dress, a calamity to which Joan also brought my attention. I'm wondering if she is manifesting these emergencies. "Joan," I say. "Did you do ketamine in there?"

Through the closed door of the women's break room, we hear hemming, grousing.

"Call the police," she says. "Tell them we were doing inventory and found a tiger in the break room. Wait," she interrupts herself. "If they come here, will they shoot her?"

"How do you know it's a she?"

"She's in the women's break room," Joan says. "At least a they."

"What do we do if we don't call someone?"

Joan exhales and makes a pronouncement, leaving a warehouse of silence between each word. "We could . . . go home?"

"And leave it for the morning shift?" I say. "They complain when there's leftover folding."

A roar from the dressing room. Joan gathers her wallet and phone into her bag as I shut off the lights.


The next morning, there is no news on any of the local channels about a tiger-related massacre. I bring two coffees to work and meet Joan in the parking lot.

Mandee's is buzzing with early shoppers. We are silent as we walk inside to find the morning shift looking annoyed.

"The hangers were a mess when we got here," the morning manager says. "It took an hour to untangle them!"

"Is that all?" I say, and she says, "What do you mean, is that all? Is there something else?"

"You tell us," Joan says.

The women's break room is in order. A few of our coworkers sit at the plastic tables eating soup.

At the end of our shift, Joan and I sit in her car. The rumbling of the dressing room walls, its bitching, the roar. "Technically, we never saw the tiger, so it may have never existed," I say.

"It was there," Joan insists. "I saw its paws and stripes."

We gaze over the lot to the doors of the warehouse, sliding open to permit a family.

My mother grows stronger. She can yank the hose around the *my heart burns* and *sincerity* and will soon be ready to drive again. We celebrate her health by ordering two combination platters at the Chinese restaurant for pickup.

"Pork fried rice," she reminds me, nervous they'll forget.

"I told them twice," I said.

We drive over in her boxy car. The Cadillac of go-karts.

In the vestibule of the Chinese restaurant, people read enormous menus. The man who asked if I wanted to see him masturbate eats dinner in the dining room with what looks like his family. A woman and a boy. I think of my friend's daughters peering out from the webbed shade of the screen door. The aluminum sneeze when it snaps back, the cheap, measly circumstances that trap them.

"Wait here," I tell my mom.

I walk into the dining room and stand above the man. Seeing me, he pales, looks around, as if expecting a surprise film crew. I try to say masturbate. I open my mouth.

The woman says, "Hon?"

"Look," he says, as if to reason with me.

His boy squirms in his seat, but I won't let go of anything at this table. "Dad?" The boy shares an exclamation point of a forehead with the man.

I try to say: truck. I stand over them for what feels like a long time. The family beneath me arranged in a pathetic tableau, the son looks at the man who looks at his hands. A waitress behind me holds a tray of fat-glassed waters. "Ma'am?"

In the vestibule my mother clutches our steaming bag. I check the containers.

"Pork fried rice city," I assure her.

We stop into the pharmacy, where I try on the same sunglasses I've tried on all summer and my mother buys an entertainment magazine with Taylor Swift on the cover.

The face of the truck man's wife had changed the instant I approached. She may not have known the shape, but she knew something was coming. I hope she will ask him a series of bruising questions but, knowing how things go, figure she probably won't. Some people turn in whatever direction allows them to see what they want.

As we walk to the car, I fill my mother in on my friend's boyfriend. How their truck has to be rigged with a court-ordered Breathalyzer. How it's a bulky, ugly device that humiliates my friend who also has to use it when she drives her girls.

The man in the truck who asked me to watch him masturbate is not the wildest part of the summer. Neither is the lady stuck in her dress or even the tiger. The wildest part is what happens when my mother and I get to the car.

We secure the takeout in the back seat and are buckling our seat belts up front when she makes an announcement: "I'm going to say something and you're not going to like it."

I pause, key hovering by the ignition. "Say it."

"I don't know why I'm supposed to care about Taylor Swift's private life. Tell me instead about a woman struggling to work a job and raise kind kids."

"That's whose private life you want to know about?"

She claps to rid her hands of imaginary dust: *that's all.*

The key doesn't fit in the ignition. I try again. "This key isn't working," I say.

My mother pages through the magazine. "What's wrong with it?"

I realize that the rearview mirror is positioned to a different person's parameters at the same time my mother says, "Whose kid's seat is that?"

In the back seat, a stuffed starfish and a discarded sippy cup.

My mother makes a second announcement: "This is not our car." We've loaded our food and buckled ourselves into another person's midsize sedan the same color and make as hers, whose owner exhibited the same trust or carelessness by not locking the doors. My mother points through the windshield to our car, a few yards away. It is startling to see the thing you think you're sitting inside. We are laughing so hard we can barely get out and walk to the correct car. Once there, we realize we've forgotten the food. I return to the other car and retrieve our combination platters, trailed by the sensation of stealing.

In the correct car my mother and I thumb tears from our

eyes. The key works, which makes us laugh harder. We pull out of the lot, staring at the incorrect car in wonder.

"Who was that man in the restaurant?" my mother wants to know when we get on the road.

"An old bandmate."

"You're not going to tell me." She shifts to watch the passing fields and I wonder if she is angry until she says, laughing again, "So busy talking we got into the wrong car."

At the end of the month, I will move to the city and get a job taping small pieces of paper to larger pieces of paper to be fed through an industrial printer. In a few months, I will get promoted and become the person who feeds the paper into the machine until the company goes out of business and I spend a few years working temp jobs and dating an actor who perpetually looks like he is on the verge of epiphany and will never say anything that makes me laugh. One night, disgusted by him and his friends, I'll invent a list of grievances then stand alone in front of a mirror. "You're a heartbreaker," I will say, then ask myself, "How do you know?" and answer myself, "Just look at you!"

My mother will continue to live in that house, walking two extra rooms to throw out a Q-tip and ignoring her health problems. We will see each other twice a year, not because of animosity but because of life. But driving home that night, dinner steaming in the back seat, my throat constricts when I think of leaving. I'd grown to enjoy preparing her sandwiches. Carrying her to bed, her soft hands folded around my neck as I lower her onto the sheets I laundered. Clipping the zinnia heads; relieving them of what's not working so they can concentrate on what is.

Guiding the hose away from the fern's tender stalks. Adding sugar water to the hummingbird feeder. Replacing flowers in the vase. Changing, opening, adding. Sacred acts I can rely on. I like that my presence adds dignity. Every morning I open the blinds to the gulls and the bay muck, and every night the sun sets over the lawn filled with fathers.

What I like most is the moment before she opens her bedroom door, the gulls circling the sandbars, the blink and the coffee chug, the gulls and muck, the inside and out, even the fears of the crab in the shallow inlet, the understanding that everything shifts to something else until there is no more shifting. Of course, two people—one!—can be a family. What's more surprising is that you can have a private relationship with time.

The reason the man in the truck, the stuck dress, and the tiger weren't as wild as the wrong car is because they were acts that happened to us. Getting into the wrong car felt like something my mother and I enacted. Like we'd stumbled onto a mystery. That it turned out to be a simple mistake only made the mystery wider. But it was generated by us. Our conversation. Our love.

# Viola in Midwinter

◯

The Margaretville Shop & Save stays open twenty-four hours as a service to hunters, hospital employees, sex workers, and other creatures who work at night. Viola in predawn debates poppers and pharaoh snakes in the fireworks aisle. In the checkout line, hunters discuss a bobcat one saw on his drive into town. A mama, probably, looking for food before the real snow arrives and locks the county in place. Seeing Viola, their voices zip. She knows they call her Dark Lady which she sometimes enjoys. The cashier rings her purchases (poppers, a small axe, mint tea for sleep), still talking to the men collected under the announcement board though they've gone silent. They watch her pay and leave, her puffed black coat trailing like a cold remark. A numbness in her forehead framed in pain, a cricketing in the temple. She is always on the verge of a headache; the Shop & Save is always open; she is always forty-nine.

Outside, pale light crowns the higher mountain peaks though the parking lot is dark. Other hunters low under a streetlight. Viola positions her bags in the trunk, overhearing ideas in their mumblings, *I was going to*, *she would*, until one of the men, emboldened by her lack of attention, calls out. "Need help?"

She keeps her gaze on him and swings the trunk closed.

"Trying to say hi," he says.

"Being polite," his friend adds.

She pulls a cigarette from a pocket and pauses as if waiting for a light, an extinct ritual from a former life. The men blink. She finds a lighter in another pocket.

The original hunter seems to decide the smoke is meant to anger him and blooms. "Where you from?" he says. "Not here."

She exhales smoke toward where they move from foot to foot like deer that cannot smell the origin of disturbance. The Shop & Save doors whistle. A man wearing hospital scrubs emerges carrying groceries. He walks toward a different part of the lot then seeing them changes course for the encounter that had, for the men, changed from something they understood.

"Everything okay?" the EMT asks her. Blank eyes. Poised posture.

Viola spits loose tobacco onto the ground.

He turns to the men. "Everything okay?"

They push one of their own forward, a lantern thrown in front. "Just being friendly," he says.

Viola uses this interruption as cover to get in and start the car. The men move aside. The EMT stands under the streetlamp, holding his bags. She watches him in the rearview mirror. Do-gooder, maybe. She takes the road that leads into the foothills and parks near the woods she heard the men discussing.

Viola follows the tracks down the county road, in and out of the tree line until it jags into an embankment by the creek. Another awareness grows alongside hers as she walks, royal blue and not solitary. The bobcat is pregnant, Viola thinks, watching it move down the frozen stream, slow and exposed. It must be injured, but there is no blood on the trail. She follows, avoiding the mud crust whose sound would betray her. The movement of a cat's shoulders out of sequence with its forward motion pleases her. The cat slips on its way up the other bank. Her grasp is firm. She pushes a blade into its neck.

A pink dawn, flurries beginning. The animal draped like a bride over her legs. Viola sits in the snow and drinks.


Viola was forty-nine in 1917 when she met the woman who would immortalize her. Viola's husband, a temperless Swede, was fighting in France. Their seven-year-old daughter Bea had been good-natured before her father left, but now it was like living with a gathering storm. Always some petulant, bruising remark, a brush hurtling through the air. Every morning Viola left for the factory, buoyant with relief. She loved the simple purpose of a job.

The neighbors viewed her with suspicion for waiting until thirty to wed. She preferred the factory women who discussed how they'd shore up the line better than that sack of shit Haig, and, at the end of sweat-ridden shifts, how they missed their husbands rarely if at all. Under the factory's wasting lights Viola met more kinds of women than she knew existed. One or two were married to hitters and joked that these years were the clearest their faces had been. Viola didn't know women could speak so candidly, but she'd never been among so many, protected by war's isolation.

Samarra was the pinnacle of that candor. Her administrative role at the factory allowed her to walk the line and chat. Her wide, expressive mouth made everything she said sound scandalous even when she let the younger girls go to catch some school.

She befriended Viola and her storm-cloud daughter, bringing them food and clothes they could never afford. During the summer of 1917, they'd drink Samarra's whiskey in Viola's cold-water walk-up, the smell of the fish market souring through the windows. Fanning themselves only deepened the stink, but it made them laugh. Their friendship loosened whatever fist always seemed to grip Viola's chest. She confessed to Samarra that a longing rose inside her whenever she walked a street with a view of the river. Sometimes she feared it would split her in two.

Samarra said she knew a way to lessen that woe. She called it the Occupation. Typically, the conversion procedure was harder for women. The men could bite each other on the neck but women had to receive permission. The subject had to be certain.

A week after the hunters, the EMT approaches Viola in the Shop & Save.

"I'd love to know your name," he says. "So the next time those guys bother you I can at least say, 'Hey, don't bother . . .'" In the moment that passes, his smile reconsiders then strengthens. "This is where you say your name," he says.

"Men aren't new to me," she says. She says, "Viola."

He retreats a few glancing steps, pretending to be moved by beauty. It is meant to be corny. She smiles, in spite of herself. His basket is filled with honey, bread, and yogurt. Soft, sweetening things.

Outside they load her car. "How many fireworks does a woman need?" he says.

"You never know when I'll need to shove one up a hunter's ass."

He laughs, apologizes for the hunters as if he is their supervisor. He has already drawn the line between her and the town she's lived in for half a century. She says, "I've been through it before."

"Ten times today, I bet."

"A hundred."

She likes that he laughs when she curses. His hands look strong and soft and while he speaks one rests on his lower stomach. She knows it is where he wants to touch her.

Later, Viola watches him park in front of her property. He is not a stand-up-straight man but hovers lower in his body; the glancing steps at the Shop & Save and these chastened ones crossing her lawn as if clearing a series of boughs. He's young, relatively speaking, mid-forties maybe, but like many white men in middle age he looks floured, older. Viola waits for him on her porch and asks what he thinks of her house.

He makes a show of considering. "The yellow and white reminds me of my grandparents' cottage. We spent summers swimming in a stream like yours."

"You see the stream?" She is pleased.

"It's running a bit low. But it's healthy," he hastens to add. "Beavers are working it, that's a good sign. I didn't know it came out this far. And so loud."

"You hear it too?" Noting his confused look, she explains, "Sometimes I think only I can see how pretty it is here."

"How long have you lived up here?"

"Forever."

She tells him that every night more icicles grow from the gutters, and he says it's because the house isn't properly winterized. "You're not protected."

She doesn't offer him dinner. They sit on the couch with tumblers of whiskey. She asks what it's like to be an EMT and he says it's a lot of waiting until it's not. He says he has healer hands and she says, "You have healer hands," so he hears how ridiculous it sounds. He asks to touch her. She places the glass on the table, removes her sweater, and lies on the carpet. This seems to cue a tuxedo cat who comes around to sniff. She motions for it to leave.

The EMT drains his drink and crouches near her. She is pleased that he seems cowed by the sudden exposure of her skin. He places his palms against her back. When was the last time anyone touched her? He digs in with his fingertips, beginning at her spine's base. She has what he calls an ancient coil in her lower right back where she keeps people she loves. She dislikes so-called healers but dislikes more that he's right.

"I'll make you a steak for your trouble," she tells him after.

"You cook?" He gestures to her kitchen, the sink and counters covered in plants.

Viola sets one place at her table and prepares the meat on an outside pit. She serves the steak, pours herself more whiskey, and sits across from him.

"You're not going to eat?"

"Not hungry," she says.

He cuts a forkful and swears that the area's hunting helps its animals.

"A progressive and a hunter?" she says.

"There's no way around the body craving meat."

"The body craves protein, not a sirloin filet. The animal prefers to live. I'm too old to pretend."

"You're so old." He grins.

"Middle aged."

"I'm middle aged too." He seems happy to be connected by this. "You're not a vegan, are you?"

She says, "I'm a hunter too."

He removes his shirt and jeans. She sits astride him on the couch. He drags a flat tongue over her breasts. He whispers, pushing into her, that he wants to build her a house. She doesn't want him to build her a house but doesn't mind the sentiment. It's been decades since someone has pressed their cheek against her heart and shuddered against her.


On the night Viola ceased to age, she'd received a letter from her husband in France, outlining his plan for return. They'd move in with his family. She would quit the factory. It angered Bea that he mentioned the thickness of the fighting, the ranks obliterated by rot and illness but not her, not once. She spat food, threw her plate until, exhausted, lay in the back bedroom performing occasional, pitiful whimpers. Viola and Samarra shared a bottle of rye on the fire escape. Viola was grateful for Samarra's company. She'd never seen a woman move through a room like a cleaver.

"It's hard to be forgotten by a man," Samarra said about Bea.

"She doesn't realize the letter sounds like it does because he's scared and not admitting it."

The rye worked her mood loose until the fish stink seemed participatory. She asked about the Occupation. Samarra said that inability to handle sunlight was a myth. It was more of a strong aversion that had been exaggerated by men who couldn't handle it. "Like most things, the truth has contradictions that don't fit neat theories," she said. "We don't turn to ash. We've just usually had long nights and are nursing plasma hangovers."

Human blood was not the only way to receive sustenance. They could hunt animals, though Samarra considered this beneath her. She was raised by maids in the Philippines in an affluent diplomat family. She made deals with meat factory bosses and had first pick after the slaughter. "You'd be surprised how easy it is for an older woman to go unnoticed. They either assume I have a family somewhere or I'm there to clean."

The war was ending. Survivors were coming home. After her husband returned, Viola would spend every day with his mother and sisters, mending, darning, keeping polite. Samarra reached over and untied the top of Viola's dress. Viola felt the chill of her skin meeting air. Samarra pressed her lips against her neck, pushed her fingers inside Viola. The feeling made Viola want to choose something for the rest of her life.

"Are you sure?" Samarra said, and Viola said, "Please, yes."

The EMT does not leave in the morning but chooses a contemporary short story collection from her library to read to her. The next day, he works his hospital shift and returns with a bag of groceries. Flowers, mint, salt. She places her lips against the hollow of his collarbone. He works another night shift. She goes with him: new love makes joining someone at work seem fun. He opens a wall-size cabinet revealing racks of blood, shining in bags. A genital pulse overwhelms her, her vision pinwheels. He holds her up against a wall during sex. He pulls a hammock from the attic and hangs it outside. She watches him from the shadows on the porch. The sun makes his eyes go clear. He leans against a pine, stretches each arm overhead. The crescent of pellucid skin above his belt adds itself to the night shifts and blurs time. She doesn't know how many nights have passed since the first when she made him a steak. She likes rubbing moisturizer she doesn't need into her cheeks while he reads in the other room. Viola writhes, cries out, fixed in place by the softest pin. The joy of having a tongue inside her that knows what it's doing.

"It's not fair," she says, meaning: *Thank god life can still hold this joy.*

Samarra would call this "love jail." Viola thinks she knows how it feels to wear nothing and lie beneath the sun.


In the waning days of war, Viola's new appetite became a second body. In the pale, drenched moments before satiation she could watch it as if she were a bystander. How it swerved and knuckled down on an unsuspecting figure. She engaged in nocturnal benders that ended at Samarra's apartment, where she stopped herself in ice baths.

Plague shuttered the city. A telegram from France arrived. Her husband was missing. Bea retreated into the room of herself where Viola became a foe.

Viola was the oldest she'd ever be and no longer needed food. She registered the loss of her husband in an unlit part of her brain. She was a novice immortal and though Samarra was a veteran she was unwilling to teach. She didn't want to explain, for example, why Viola's longing to leave had not lessened but hardened. They hadn't anticipated that the Occupation plus Viola's age would combine to quadruple desire. Samarra was in her sixties, safely beyond middle age. They didn't argue but backed away from one another.

Viola and the EMT hunt.

His gear and blinds amuse her. He lines up a shot to find she's been streaming in from another direction. Both methods prove effective. Bodies pile up. Their love is bad for the animals.

Showing off is new to her, as is someone anticipating her tricks. Even in deepest cover, he finds her. If you think you're being watched, he says, you are.

One night, a whiff of impermanence makes her crave concrete answers. Does he want to stay with her? No town? No job? Just his body and hers. There is a way, but he must be certain. "It will be for a long time."

The future tense makes him grow still—a squirrel sensing movement freezing at the base of an oak—until she doesn't know what is him and what is tree. She thought she'd been following the path of their desire. He makes an excuse and leaves.

Though Viola's aging halted, other parts advanced. Her hair and nails grew so fast she could shave her head and have floor-length hair within weeks. Menstrual blood disappeared for months then, as if to compensate, returned with painful hemorrhaging. No longer able to care for Bea, Viola took her to live with her Swedish relatives. At sixteen, Bea began work as a boardinghouse waitress.

One evening in the middle of the century, mother and daughter passed each other on the street. It took Viola a moment to understand that this hard woman was her daughter. Bea had exceeded her in age and looked to be in failing health. Viola realized that the girl with her was Bea's daughter, who'd inherited her grandmother's lavender eyes. Bea belonged to another time that moved like a barge away from where Viola was pinned to the dock. She'd already forgotten Bea's birthday and her own. Split with regret, she left the city.

In the 1960s, Viola worked as a flight attendant. She hunted in the Scottish Highlands, prowled the bars in Golden Gai. For a while travel allayed her restlessness. Samarra was right about one thing—it was easy for a middle-aged woman to go unnoticed. The other flight attendants were on their own thresholds—after college, before marriage, before babies, after raising children, post-divorce, post-widowhood, after changing careers, before retirement.

But a sensation of vanishing pursued Viola. She worried that instead of being freed, she'd been forgotten. She longed for her chin to sag, any indication she was still alive. Perhaps this was why people invested in religion or children or causes. To pass time pleasantly while watching something grow. Instead, Viola noticed how human tendencies genuflected through time. Hemlines and mothering trends advanced and receded. The tendency of women to wound their own. The child became the nucleus of the house, they even had their own room for toys. It sickened Viola to watch mothers be controlled by toddlers.

At the turn of the century, the idea of youth broadened to include the forties. Viola's body seemed newly valued. Men's gazes, once trained solely on college-age asses, lingered on hers. Factories, planes, space travel, the internet. Though the structures varied, they were built from hubris. Stitched with greed.

New mandates after 9/11 required flight attendants to submit to regular reviews, and Viola could no longer fly with anonymity. She returned to America and moved to the Western Catskills, where she spent her days in and out of hot flashes, chased by an unleavened smell, fertile and not, fertile then not, joints swelling, trapped in a developmental doorway. She kept routines she did not need, like market shopping to tend the last ember of being human, and lived timelessly in the woods that were silenced by snow for half of every year. She'd been middle-aged for a century, intuitions deepening, minor and major knives growing along the walls of her understanding. She was a cave purpled with stalactites. She could smell feelings in a room.

The EMT shows up after two weeks, carrying chanterelles he's foraged. Viola participates with a few bites. Worm-thick, spiced by earth. Since it serves no purpose, food is something she understands but doesn't enjoy, like perfume and holidays.

"What do you do for fun?" He seems distracted. The question belongs to an earlier stage of courtship, like he is returning to an improperly filled out form to correct mistakes.

She shows him her arsenal of fireworks and he lines up an impressive display. Colorful sparks soar above the woods. A tornado of snapping around their ankles.

"I'm surprised you don't get noise complaints," he says, gazing over the trees toward town. She notices a stab of effort in his voice, as if trying to recall what brought him here.

"No one would come all the way out."

She's been with locals before, though none from his genera-
tion. A dirt farmer with soft hands. His wife. Two brother lawyers. Their wives. Her favorite was a married salesman who she
saw for a year before his shame grew too large. Occasionally he
slows on her road—elderly but still possessing the same dazed,
blinking calm—trying to determine her house amid whatever
vision appears. But she never loved him, or the others, or even
Samarra. She never lost breath when leaving them, or when they
stayed away too long.


In the 1960s, Viola was traveling through the Midi-Pyrénées
when she met a cunning woman who taught her the spell to
glamour homes.

If what appeared to the visitor was a pleasant memory, they'd
get along. If it was troubling, the connection wouldn't last. One
lawyer she'd been excited about was startled back into his car by
whatever he saw. She never had a chance to ask. His bumper took
a chunk out of her hedgerow when he roared away. Most guests
couldn't see the stream, the feature that was dearest to her. Powered by some relentless turbine, every so often it would produce a
cherubic beaver, moving its weight front to back over a lichen-
thick rock. Before she met the EMT, these rare sightings had
been the highest delight of her endless life.


A week, a month, no visits. Viola finds him in the home of a local
bartender. Their bodies are pearlized in television light as he
pumps into her, whispering. Maybe this is the woman who wants

him to build her a house, Viola thinks, hovering outside the window.

She drags her firework arsenal to the lawn and lights each one. The sky fills with fury. Sparks ignite in the dusky growth. The arriving firemen cannot find a house but hear laughter spiraling in the hollow. A centuries-old hemlock falls, bisecting the county road and causing a complicated detour the locals resent.

Heartbreak slows the hours as months creak by. Viola's hair grows past the floor. She dyes it Lights Out black from a Shop & Save kit. Doubles up on face creams she doesn't need. The memory of her birthday returns. She spends November 15 shivering in a scalding bath. She cloaks her house so he'll find only ankle-breaking ruts if he tries to visit. Adds a few cats to her home and one tall dog named Oberon who stands like a masthead in the yard, every so often conjuring a single, day-splitting bark.

When she was still new to the mountains, Viola came across Death on a train platform in Arkville. Death wore an impeccable hoodie under an acid-washed blazer and stood beside an elegant suitcase, checking a timepiece. Sensing Viola's stare, she looked over. Her gaze was a climate. She raised a delicate hand and saluted.

Viola returned the gesture. They were workers who shared a commute. She wondered if they could be friends since neither needed anything from the other. It must get lonely being that essential. Viola thought she knew how that felt. The train arrived. Viola watched Death move through the car of sleeping travelers. She selected a window seat, removed her watch, and gently laid it on the tray table in front of her. No passenger stirred. No one notices remarkable women.

Viola watched the train leave then bought a newspaper and a bottle of pills that promised to alleviate the ankle swelling that accompanied her like an assistant.

A little boy gapes in the Shop & Save's firearms aisle where Viola wears remnants from her past lives. A corset shows under a one-shouldered dress from the 1980s belted in the style of the '90s. Flapper gloves. Bobby socks. Boots from her first life's job.

She misses the factory. She misses the women who sneaked flasks, spit seeds, bit, demurred to the bosses then exposed their asses for laughs. She hadn't known there were women like that. Since then, she has been them all.

The little boy's mother snatches him away, but he wants to keep looking at the Dark Lady.

Viola points one glowing shoulder at him, shows her teeth. Then zips it all—her mirth and misery—under the purple coat and leaves through the whistling doors.

That evening, Viola wakes, struggling for breath. Her sheets are soaked in sweat. The wind swirling in the hollow sounds like a passing big rig. Gunpowder fills her nostrils. No one is in the meadow blanketed with snow, or on the hill milked in the waxing Wolf Moon. No deer lolls in the copse of hemlock that stubbles the crest. More icicles have grown from the gutters. One side of the house shines in the dark.

Viola repots plants in her kitchen, uneasiness growing. Though she cannot die, it's still no fun to be menaced. Finally, she feels a presence behind her.

"Devour me," it says.

Samarra stands in the center of the room, arms raised for a hug. She is in town to check out the "whole upstate thing."

"Girl," she says. "You look rough."

"I could use a party," Viola admits.

"You could use a haircut. No matter. Party's here, babe."

They are naked for days. They throw a log into the fire. They finish the whiskey.

Samarra, addressing Viola from between her legs, tells her the word for the EMT is *narcissist*. "My seventh—no, eighth!—husband was one. Diminishing returns. They leave you starving." She laughs. "Which is the worst thing you and I can be."

"What did you do to him?" Viola says.

"Poor man. He did not go easy."

Samarra suggests they kill the EMT too but Viola refuses. Killing him would bring no relief, she says.

"Well, I'm going to have to eat something," Samarra says. "I'm not here to ski."

"I know a place," Viola says.

They drive to the Shop & Save and chuck tote bags and firewood into a jangling cart. Samarra humps the bear statue and tries on fluorescent hunting gear. It is good to be with this unruly woman in a cheap grocery store at night. They've been friends for a hundred years.

When they'd arrived the parking lot was empty, but when

they load their bags into the car hunters watch from under every streetlamp.

"Hello, boys," Samarra calls, driving away.

Viola directs her to the unmarked door at the back of the hospital. She leads them through a series of hallways, avoiding night nurses who glimmer in deeper rooms. Viola reveals the cabinet of blood.

Samarra leans on the counter for support. "Why do I have the urge to bless myself?"

They fill the tote bags, retreat through the hallways, and load the car.

"Hurry," Viola says when she hears someone behind them. Samarra climbs into the car.

"Wait." The EMT approaches, face mapped with pain. "Talk to me, Viola. Why have you disappeared?"

"Babe?" Samarra lowers the window and observes him with flat gray eyes. Her pallor has been flawless for centuries.

"Who's that?" he says. "Who is that?"

"That's the guy?" Samarra says when they drive away. "You need to leave the woods more."


Samarra predicts the EMT will show up again and, on a moonless night in midwinter, he does.

Viola reveals her house (she's been drinking). He stands on the porch and speaks quietly into the closed door while on the other side she listens in the dark, Oberon beside her keeping a low growl. She watches him walk to his truck. His headlights scan her as he pulls away.

Viola drains every fisher-cat on the mountain.

The EMT takes up with another local girl, homely with pretty eyes. Another progressive who insists that hunting is fair to the animal and who defers to him, unlike the bartender he keeps fucking even after he and the pretty girl marry.

They have two boys, indistinguishable from the other county kids. One moves to Canada, the other marries a local girl like his mother, hunts with his father on weekends, pulls the sightless deer onto the car, sings down the mountain. Every year the EMT decorates their house with blow-up snowmen. His property backs onto an overgrown section of woods that connects the hamlet.

One night toward the middle of the century, the EMT grills meat in his backyard. He is in his seventies, lymph nodes stuffed with cancer. She smells it coursing above the char: metallic, salted. It seems unfair that he gets to die.

A windless rustle, a certain un-sound. He doesn't have to see her standing inside the tree line, owl quiet, to know.


She meets him again, in this town or that, a man or not, sick or well, a doctor, a stoneworker, and he runs his systems on her. Sometimes, she doesn't have the energy. She tells him she's been through it before. Sometimes, she accepts his dances, his tongue, attempts to summon love's old frictions until, inevitably, the drumming subsides.


A girl on the verge of adulthood arrives in November, when the forest's reddish growth makes the mountains appear rusted. She has compiled a map from four semi-accurate ones procured in visits to town hall. She has sweet-talked a hunter who liked her lavender eyes. This determination, paired with a hard countenance, has separated her from everyone she's ever known. The girl walks onto the empty meadow and the word *ancestor* occurs to her as if from clear air. Each step presses it into the moss. *Ancestor*, she feels the Devonian gaze of hemlocks. *Ancestor*, the rocks that pin the stream. She scolds her hammering heart (the house will arrive or it won't and if it doesn't she'll just go home). Nothing in her life has prompted such breathlessness. Something in the meadow seems to unlock and turn toward her. The stream begins a louder chatter—it sounds like it's saying hello. I won't leave. I'll wait forever.

# Acknowledgments

For their care with the author and/or the stories of *Exit Zero*, vast gratitude to Claudia Ballard, Jenna Johnson, Lianna Culp, Thomas Colligan, and the entire team at Farrar, Straus and Giroux and Picador. Phyllis Trout and Brian Brooks, Julia Strayer, the Munster Literature Centre in Cork, Ireland, the Ragdale Foundation, and Yale University's English and Creative Writing Departments.

These gentle editors: Tiffany Gibert (*Time Out*), Julia Brown (*Gulf Coast*), Michael Koch (*Epoch*), Ben Samuel (*BOMB*), Emma Komlos-Hrobsky (*Tin House*), Thomas Morris (*Stinging Fly*), Manuel Gonzales (*Bennington Review*), Heidi Pitlor and Lauren Groff (*The Best American Short Stories*), and Laura Furman (PEN/O. Henry Prizes). Adeena Reitberger, Amanda Faraone, and Rebecca Markovits at *American Short Fiction*. Drew Broussard, Dan Sheehan, Téa Obreht, and Halimah Marcus and *Electric Literature*, thank you.

My lodestars: Edward P. Jones, Yoko Ogawa, Aimee Bender, Amy Hempel, Adolfo Bioy Casares, Toni Morrison. The bratty _____ that maintains its unsayability. It's a life honor to try to articulate it, fail, and try again. How Maryrose Nowak always says, "You don't see why not." The Catskill Mountains, the deep dark woods, the blue-black sea. Every boss I've ever had who, whether they knew it or liked it, paid me to write.

My community of writers, readers, students, teachers, brothers, friends, family. The Dodson family, especially Tommy, Marianne, and Leah. Helene Bertino, who let me paint on the walls. Marcello, Merlin, and my partner, the poet Ted Dodson, whose uncompromising work keeps mine honest.

I'd like to remember my Uncle Joe, who was a submarine cook—world's coolest job. When I was little, he carved a radish into a rose for me. It was the most magical thing I'd ever seen, and still is.